外语教学指导与学术研究系列丛书

英美文学名家经典作品简析

A Brief Analysis of British and American Celebrated Writers' Classical Works

刘赢南　张传宏　王建光
温　泉　黄　吟　编　著

北京理工大学出版社
BEIJING INSTITUTE OF TECHNOLOGY PRESS

图书在版编目（CIP）数据

英美文学名家经典作品简析：英文/刘赢南等编著．—北京：北京理工大学出版社，2015.12

ISBN 978－7－5682－1569－5

Ⅰ.①英…　Ⅱ.①刘…　Ⅲ.①英国文学－文学评论－英文②文学评论－美国－英文　Ⅳ.①I561.06　②I712.06

中国版本图书馆CIP数据核字（2015）第299114号

出版发行／北京理工大学出版社有限责任公司
社　　址／北京市海淀区中关村南大街5号
邮　　编／100081
电　　话／(010) 68914775（总编室）
　　　　82562903（教材售后服务热线）
　　　　68948351（其他图书服务热线）
网　　址／http：//www.bitpress.com.cn
经　　销／全国各地新华书店
印　　刷／保定市中画美凯印刷有限公司
开　　本／710毫米×1000毫米　1/16
印　　张／7.25
字　　数／100千字
版　　次／2015年12月第1版　2015年12月第1次印刷
定　　价／28.00元

责任编辑／武丽娟
文案编辑／武丽娟
责任校对／周瑞红
责任印制／王美丽

前　言

《英美文学名家经典作品赏析》是一本囊括英美近现代多位著名作家数篇著名作品、作家概述及作品简析的书籍。此书的编著旨在提高广大文学爱好者的文学鉴赏力，特别是英美文学鉴赏能力，把握英美文学发展脉络，提高文学分析与批评能力，近而了解现当代英美文化与社会。

《英美文学名家经典作品赏析》共分三个部分：①作家概述 ②作品导读与简析 ③作品原文。该书选自英美近现代的著名作品，它们内涵丰富，贴近生活，时代感强，语言通俗易懂，非常具有可读性。

作　者

2015 年 8 月

Contents

I

Edgar Allan Poe

1.1 The Introductory Remarks of Edgar Allan Poe

Edgar Allan Poe is the celebrated American literary critic, famous romantic poet and forerunner of American detective story. His life is a tragic one, and thus such tragic life has formed his unique writing style and meditative theme. Poe's poetic theory exerts great influence on the poets and writers after him.

Edgar Allan Poe was born in a humble family. When he was about four years old, both his parents died. He became an orphan. Later a rich Diamond businessman adopted him. In Mr. Poe's family, Poe has lived a comfortable life for several years. Then he attended University of Virginia, but there appeared a severe quarrel between Mr. Allan and Poe, because Poe intended to major in literature, while Mr. Allan would like Poe to study law. This quarrel led to such outcome that Mr. Allan refused to pay tuition for Poe, so that Poe was eliminated from university. The adopted son broke up any relation with Mr. Allan. Afterwards, Poe enrolled the American Army. Soon he was sent to The West Point. Because of his gambling and drinking behavior, Poe was sent away from The West Point, so he had to earn his living as a freelancer. In 1835, he worked for The American Southern Literary Message as an editor. He published his important collection of story, *The Tales of Grotesque and Arabiansque*. Also for the sake of his ill behavior, he was fired. After he married his thirteen-year-old cousin, he came back to The American Southern Literary Message again. In 1845, he published his important collection of poetry *The Raven*. In 1847, his young wife died. Two years later, he died and his body was found in a gutter.

Edgar Allan Poe creates a lot of beautiful, but rather sorrowful poems. His beautiful and emotional pattern of poetry fascinates many readers. His horrible and mysterious detective stories form a kind of horrible beauty which deeply attracts people.

1.2 Comment on *The Purloined Letter*

Edgar Allan Poe is viewed as not only the eminent romantic poet, but also an excellent short story teller. His short stories are featured with the complex plots, eccentric characterization, horrific scenes and mysterious hue. His detective story is thought of as the classics in the world literature. Poe's short story writing style is modelled by the late generation of writers after him. *The Purloined Letter* is one of his well-known detective stories. The story tells a queer letter theft case which puzzled policemen. George, the director of police station in P city had to turn to Pain, his good friend, a private detective. After making the careful analysis of the case, Pain promised to take the purloined letter back.

The story was written in the first point of view. The narrator "I" tells the story as one of the protagonists. The conversations and dialogues among the protagonists are the main clue of the story. The story begins with the director of the police station, George's visit to the narrator and Pain, a private detective because he came across a tough trial, which is very simple superfacially, but it is very difficult to deal with. The details of the case is like this: The princess received a love letter. She was going to read it when Mrs. Duwal, the Dutchess called on her. Having considered the Dutchess had a habbit of making a gossip, the princess put the letter back into the envelope, then placed it on the table. At the same time, Mr. Lerbelon, something important in the government came in. He caught sight of the letter with the capital letter S on the envelope. He guessed that it was the princess' secret in the letter. In order to coerce the princess into supporting him in the government, Mr. Lerbelon changed her letter with his own letter. While the princess was talking with Mrs. Duwal, she found what Mr. Lerbelon had done. But she could not stop him because she was worried that Mrs. Duwal could make the news that the princess had a lover public. So she could do nothing when her letter was purloined. To find back this letter is a demanding work for George. If he could not get the letter back, he would lose his position at present. George had searched for Mr. Lerbelon's house thoroughly, but gained nothing, thus he tried to get some advice from Pain. Pain asked him the content of the letter and told him someone could give him a hand for the case. Three weeks later, George came to meet the narrator and Pain again. Pain said that he would return the purloined letter to George if he presented a prize of 50,000 francs. George agreed with him. Soon Pain took a letter from one of his drawers, which was the letter that the princess had lost. George grasped the letter with his shaking hands, reading it. Then he rose up from his seat and rushed out of the door.

Then Pain began to tell the narrator the process of how he gained the purloined letter from Mr. Lerbelon's house. One morning, Pain was wearing dark glasses to pay a visit to Mr. Lerbelon. During their talk, he was examing the room, taking notice of an ordinary shelf inserted letters. From there he saw a dirty envelope. He believed that was the princess' letter. He played a trick to get the letter from the shelf and then placed a similar letter back to the original place.

1.3 The Text of *The Purloined Letter*

Nil sapientiae odiosius acumine nimio.

Seneca.

AT Paris, just after dark one gusty evening in the autumn of 18—, I was enjoying the twofold luxury of meditation and a meerschaum, in company with my friend C. Auguste Dupin, in his little back library, or book-closet, au troisieme, No. 33, Rue Dunot, Faubourg St. Germain. For one hour at least we had maintained a profound silence; while each, to any casual observer, might have seemed intently and exclusively occupied with the curling eddies of smoke that oppressed the atmosphere of the chamber. For myself, however, I was mentally discussing certain topics which had formed matter for conversation between us at an earlier period of the evening; I mean the affair of the Rue Morgue, and the mystery attending the murder of Marie Roget. I looked upon it, therefore, as something of a coincidence, when the door of our apartment was thrown open and admitted our old acquaintance, Monsieur G—, the Prefect of the Parisian police.

We gave him a hearty welcome; for there was nearly half as much of the entertaining as of the contemptible about the man, and we had not seen him for several years. We had been sitting in the dark, and Dupin now arose for the purpose of lighting a lamp, but sat down again, without doing so, upon G.'s saying that he had called to consult us, or rather to ask the opinion of my friend, about some official business which had occasioned a great deal of trouble.

"If it is any point requiring reflection," observed Dupin, as he forbore to enkindle the wick, "we shall examine it to better purpose in the dark."

"That is another of your odd notions," said the Prefect, who had a fashion of calling every thing "odd" that was beyond his comprehension, and thus lived amid an absolute legion of "oddities."

"Very true," said Dupin, as he supplied his visitor with a pipe, and rolled towards him a comfortable chair.

"And what is the difficulty now?" I asked. "Nothing more in the assassination way, I hope?"

"Oh no; nothing of that nature. The fact is, the business is very simple indeed, and I make no doubt that we can manage it sufficiently well ourselves; but then I thought Dupin would like to hear the details of it, because it is so excessively odd."

"Simple and odd," said Dupin.

"Why, yes; and not exactly that, either. The fact is, we have all been a good deal puzzled because the affair is so simple, and yet baffles us altogether."

"Perhaps it is the very simplicity of the thing which puts you at fault," said my friend.

"What nonsense you do talk!" replied the Prefect, laughing heartily.

"Perhaps the mystery is a little too plain," said Dupin.

"Oh, good heavens! who ever heard of such an idea?"

"A little too self-evident."

"Ha! ha! ha! —ha! ha! ha! —ho! ho! ho!" —roared our visitor, profoundly amused, "oh, Dupin, you will be the death of me yet!"

"And what, after all, is the matter on hand?" I asked.

"Why, I will tell you," replied the Prefect, as he gave a long, steady, and contemplative puff, and settled himself in his chair. "I will tell you in a few words; but, before I begin, let me caution you that this is an affair demanding the greatest secrecy, and that I should most probably lose the position I now hold, were it known that I confided it to any one."

"Proceed," said I.

"Or not," said Dupin.

"Well, then; I have received personal information, from a very high quarter, that a certain document of the last importance, has been purloined from the royal apartments. The individual who purloined it is known; this beyond a doubt; he was seen to take it. It is known, also, that it still remains in his possession."

"How is this known?" asked Dupin.

"It is clearly inferred," replied the Prefect, "from the nature of the document, and from the nonappearance of certain results which would at once arise from its passing out of the robber's possession; —that is to say, from his employing it as he must design in the end to employ it."

"Be a little more explicit," I said.

"Well, I may venture so far as to say that the paper gives its holder a certain power in a certain quarter where such power is immensely valuable." The Prefect was fond of the cant of diplomacy.

"Still I do not quite understand," said Dupin.

"No? Well; the disclosure of the document to a third person, who shall be nameless, would bring in question the honor of a personage of most exalted station; and this fact gives the holder of the document an ascendancy over the illustrious personage whose honor and peace are so jeopardized."

"But this ascendancy," I interposed, "would depend upon the robber's knowledge of the loser's knowledge of the robber. Who would dare—"

"The thief," said G., "is the Minister D—, who dares all things, those unbecoming as well as those becoming a man. The method of the theft was not less ingenious than bold. The document in question —a letter, to be frank —had been received by the personage robbed while alone in the royal boudoir. During its perusal she was suddenly interrupted by the entrance of the other exalted personage from whom especially it was her wish to conceal it. After a hurried and vain endeavor to thrust it in a drawer, she was forced to place it, open as it was, upon a table. The address, however, was uppermost, and, the contents thus unexposed, the letter escaped notice. At this juncture enters the Minister D—. His lynx eye immediately perceives the paper, recognises the handwriting of the address, observes the confusion of the personage addressed, and fathoms her secret. After some business transactions, hurried through in his ordinary manner, he produces a letter somewhat similar to the one in question, opens it, pretends to read it, and then places it in close juxtaposition to the other. Again he converses, for some fifteen minutes, upon the public affairs. At length, in taking leave, he takes also from the table the letter to which he had no claim. Its rightful owner saw, but, of course, dared not call attention to the act, in the presence of the third personage who stood at her elbow. The minister decamped; leaving his own letter —one of no importance —upon the table."

"Here, then," said Dupin to me, "you have precisely what you demand to make the ascendancy complete —the robber's knowledge of the loser's knowledge of the robber."

"Yes," replied the Prefect; "and the power thus attained has, for some months past, been wielded, for political purposes, to a very dangerous extent. The personage robbed is more thoroughly convinced, every day, of the necessity of reclaiming her letter. But this, of course, cannot be done openly. In fine, driven to despair, she has committed the matter to me."

"Than whom," said Dupin, amid a perfect whirlwind of smoke, "no more sagacious agent could, I suppose, be desired, or even imagined."

"You flatter me," replied the Prefect; "but it is possible that some such opinion may have been entertained."

"It is clear," said I, "as you observe, that the letter is still in possession of the minister; since it is this possession, and not any employment of the letter, which bestows the power. With the employment the power departs."

"True," said G. "and upon this conviction I proceeded. My first care was to make thorough search of the minister's hotel; and here my chief embarrassment lay in the necessity of searching without his knowledge. Beyond all things, I have been warned of the danger which would result from giving him reason to suspect our design."

"But," said I, "you are quite au fait in these investigations. The Parisian police have done this thing often before."

"Oh yes; and for this reason I did not despair. The habits of the minister gave me, too, a great advantage. He is frequently absent from home all night. His servants are by no means numerous. They sleep at a distance from their master's apartment, and, being chiefly Neapolitans, are readily made drunk. I have keys, as you know, with which I can open any chamber or cabinet in Paris. For three months a night has not passed, during the greater part of which I have not been engaged, personally, in ransacking the D—

Hotel. My honor is interested, and, to mention a great secret, the reward is enormous. So I did not abandon the search until I had become fully satisfied that the thief is a more astute man than myself. I fancy that I have investigated every nook and corner of the premises in which it is possible that the paper can be concealed."

"But is it not possible," I suggested, "that although the letter may be in possession of the minister, as it unquestionably is, he may have concealed it elsewhere than upon his own premises?"

"This is barely possible," said Dupin. "The present peculiar condition of affairs at court, and especially of those intrigues in which D—is known to be involved, would render the instant availability of the document —its susceptibility of being produced at a moment's notice —a point of nearly equal importance with its possession."

"Its susceptibility of being produced?" said I.

"That is to say, of being destroyed," said Dupin.

"True," I observed; "the paper is clearly then upon the premises. As for its being upon the person of the minister, we may consider that as out of the question."

"Entirely," said the Prefect. "He has been twice waylaid, as if by footpads, and his person rigorously searched under my own inspection."

"You might have spared yourself this trouble," said Dupin. "D—, I presume, is not altogether a fool, and, if not, must have anticipated these waylayings, as a matter of course."

"Not altogether a fool," said G., "but then he's a poet, which I take to be only one remove from a fool."

"True," said Dupin, after a long and thoughtful whiff from his meerschaum, "although I have been guilty of certain doggerel myself."

"Suppose you detail," said I, "the particulars of your search."

"Why the fact is, we took our time, and we searched every where. I have had long experience in these affairs. I took the entire building, room by room; devoting the nights of a whole week to each. We examined, first, the furniture of each apartment. We opened every possible drawer; and I presume you know that, to a properly trained police agent, such a thing as a secret drawer is impossible. Any man is a dolt who permits a 'secret' drawer to escape him in a search of this kind. The thing is so plain. There is a certain amount of bulk —of space —to be accounted for in every cabinet. Then we have accurate rules. The fiftieth part of a line could not escape us. After the cabinets we took the chairs. The cushions we probed with the fine long needles you have seen me employ. From the tables we removed the tops."

"Why so?"

"Sometimes the top of a table, or other similarly arranged piece of furniture, is removed by the person wishing to conceal an article; then the leg is excavated, the article deposited within the cavity, and the top replaced. The bottoms and tops of bedposts are employed in the same way."

"But could not the cavity be detected by sounding?" I asked.

"By no means, if, when the article is deposited, a sufficient wadding of cotton be placed around it. Besides, in our case, we were obliged to proceed without noise."

"But you could not have removed —you could not have taken to pieces all articles of furniture in which it would have been possible to make a deposit in the manner you mention. A letter may be compressed into a thin spiral roll, not differing much in shape or bulk from a large knitting-needle, and in this form it might be inserted into the rung of a chair, for example. You did not take to pieces all the chairs?"

"Certainly not; but we did better —we examined the rungs of every chair in the hotel, and, indeed, the jointings of every description of furniture, by the aid of a most powerful microscope. Had there been any traces of recent disturbance we should not have failed to detect it instantly. A single grain of gimlet-dust, for example, would have been as obvious as an apple. Any disorder in the glueing —any unusual gaping in the joints —would have sufficed to insure detection."

"I presume you looked to the mirrors, between the boards and the plates, and you probed the beds and the bed-clothes, as well as the curtains and carpets."

"That of course; and when we had absolutely completed every particle of the furniture in this way, then we examined the house itself. We divided its entire surface into compartments, which we numbered, so that none might be missed; then we scrutinized each individual square inch throughout the premises, including the two houses immediately adjoining, with the microscope, as before."

"The two houses adjoining!" I exclaimed; "you must have had a great deal of trouble."

"We had; but the reward offered is prodigious."

"You include the grounds about the houses?"

"All the grounds are paved with brick. They gave us comparatively little trouble. We examined the moss between the bricks, and found it undisturbed."

"You looked among D—'s papers, of course, and into the books of the library?"

"Certainly; we opened every package and parcel; we not only opened every book, but we turned over every leaf in each volume, not contenting ourselves with a mere shake, according to the fashion of some of our police officers. We also measured the thickness of every book-cover, with the most accurate admeasurement, and applied to each the most jealous scrutiny of the microscope. Had any of the bindings been recently meddled with, it would have been utterly impossible that the fact should have escaped observation. Some five or six volumes, just from the hands of the binder, we carefully probed, longitudinally, with the needles."

"You explored the floors beneath the carpets?"

"Beyond doubt. We removed every carpet, and examined the boards with the microscope."

"And the paper on the walls?"

"Yes."

"You looked into the cellars?"

"We did."

"Then," I said, "you have been making a miscalculation, and the letter is not upon the premises, as you suppose."

"I fear you are right there," said the Prefect. "And now,

Dupin, what would you advise me to do?"

"To make a thorough re-search of the premises."

"That is absolutely needless," replied G—. "I am not more sure that I breathe than I am that the letter is not at the Hotel."

"I have no better advice to give you," said Dupin. "You have, of course, an accurate description of the letter?"

"Oh yes!" —And here the Prefect, producing a memorandum-book, proceeded to read aloud a minute account of the internal, and especially of the external appearance of the missing document. Soon after finishing the perusal of this description, he took his departure, more entirely depressed in spirits than I had ever known the good gentleman before.

In about a month afterwards he paid us another visit, and found us occupied very nearly as before. He took a pipe and a chair and entered into some ordinary conversation. At length I said,—

"Well, but G—, what of the purloined letter? I presume you have at last made up your mind that there is no such thing as over-reaching the Minister?"

"Confound him, say I —yes; I made the reexamination, however, as Dupin suggested —but it was all labor lost, as I knew it would be."

"How much was the reward offered, did you say?" asked Dupin.

"Why, a very great deal —a very liberal reward —I don't like to say how much, precisely; but one thing I will say, that I wouldn't mind giving my individual check for fifty thousand francs to any one who could obtain me that letter. The fact is, it is becoming of more and more importance every day; and the reward has been lately doubled. If it were trebled, however, I could do no more than I have done."

"Why, yes," said Dupin, drawlingly, between the whiffs of his meerschaum, "I really —think, G—, you have not exerted yourself—to the utmost in this matter. You might —do a little more, I think, eh?"

"How? —In what way?"

"Why —puff, puff —you might —puff, puff —employ counsel in the matter, eh? —puff, puff, puff. Do you remember the story they tell of Abernethy?"

"No; hang Abernethy!"

"To be sure! hang him and welcome. But, once upon a time, a certain rich miser conceived the design of spunging upon this Abernethy for a medical opinion. Getting up, for this purpose, an ordinary conversation in a private company, he insinuated his case to the physician, as that of an imaginary individual.

"'We will suppose,' said the miser, 'that his symptoms are such and such; now, doctor, what would you have directed him to take?'

"'take!' said Abernethy, 'why, take advice, to be sure.'"

"But," said the Prefect, a little discomposed, "I am perfectly willing to take advice, and to pay for it. I would really give fifty thousand francs to any one who would aid me in the matter."

"In that case," replied Dupin, opening a drawer, and producing a check-book, "you may as well fill me up a check for the amount mentioned. When you have signed it, I will hand you the letter."

I was astounded. The Prefect appeared absolutely thunderstricken. For some minutes he remained speechless and motionless, less, looking incredulously at my friend with open mouth, and eyes that seemed starting from their sockets; then, apparently in some measure, he seized a pen, and after several pauses and vacant stares, finally filled up and signed a check for fifty thousand francs, and handed it across the table to Dupin. The latter examined it carefully and deposited it in his pocket-book; then, unlocking an escritoire, took thence a letter and gave it to the Prefect. This functionary grasped it in a perfect agony of joy, opened it with a trembling hand, cast a rapid glance at its contents, and then, scrambling and struggling to the door, rushed at length unceremoniously from the room and from the house, without having uttered a syllable since Dupin had requested him to fill up the check.

When he had gone, my friend entered into some explanations.

"The Parisian police," he said, "are exceedingly able in their way. They are persevering, ingenious, cunning, and thoroughly versed in the knowledge which their duties seem chiefly to demand. Thus, when G—detailed to us his mode of searching the premises at the Hotel D—, I felt entire confidence in his having made a satisfactory investigation —so far as his labors extended."

"So far as his labors extended?" said I.

"Yes," said Dupin. "The measures adopted were not only the best of their kind, but carried out to absolute perfection. Had the letter been deposited within the range of their search, these fellows would, beyond a question, have found it."

I merely laughed —but he seemed quite serious in all that he said.

"The measures, then," he continued, "were good in their kind, and well executed; their defect lay in their being inapplicable to the case, and to the man. A certain set of highly ingenious resources are, with the Prefect, a sort of Procrustean bed, to which he forcibly adapts his designs. But he perpetually errs by being too deep or too shallow, for the matter in hand; and many a schoolboy is a better reasoner than he. I knew one about eight years of age, whose success at guessing in the game of 'even and odd' attracted universal admiration. This game is simple, and is played with marbles. One player holds in his hand a number of these toys, and demands of another whether that number is even or odd. If the guess is right, the guesser wins one; if wrong, he loses one. The boy to whom I allude won all the marbles of the school. Of course he had some principle of guessing; and this lay in mere observation and admeasurement of the astuteness of his opponents. For example, an arrant simpleton is his opponent, and, holding up his closed hand, asks, 'are they even or odd?' Our schoolboy replies, 'odd,' and loses; but upon the second trial he wins, for he then says to himself, 'the simpleton had them even upon the first trial, and his amount of cunning is just sufficient to make him have them odd upon the second; I will therefore guess odd;' —he guesses odd, and wins. Now, with a simpleton a degree above the first, he would have reasoned thus: 'this fellow finds that in the first instance I guessed odd, and, in the second, he will propose to himself upon the first impulse, a simple variation from even to odd, as did the first simpleton; but then a second thought will suggest that this is too simple a variation, and finally he will decide upon putting it even as before. I will therefore guess even' he guesses even, and wins. Now this mode of reasoning in the schoolboy, whom his fellows termed 'lucky,' —what, in its last analysis, is it?"

"It is merely," I said, "an identification of the reasoner's intellect with that of his opponent."

"It is," said Dupin; "and, upon inquiring of the boy by what means he effected the thorough identification in which his success consisted, I received answer as follows: 'When I wish to find out how wise, or how stupid, or how good, or how wicked is any one, or what are his thoughts at the moment, I fashion the expression of my face, as accurately as possible, in accordance with the expression of his, and then wait to see what thoughts or sentiments arise in my mind or heart, as if to match or correspond with the expression.' This response of the schoolboy lies at the bottom of all the spurious profundity which has been attributed to Rochefoucauld, to La Bougive, to Machiavelli, and to Campanella."

"And the identification," I said, "of the reasoner's intellect with that of his opponent, depends, if I understand you aright upon the accuracy with which the opponent's intellect is admeasured."

"For its practical value it depends upon this," replied Dupin; and the Prefect and his cohort fall so frequently, first, by default of this identification, and, secondly, by ill-admeasurement, or rather through non-admeasurement, of the intellect with which they are engaged. They consider only their own ideas of ingenuity; and, in searching for anything hidden, advert only to the modes in which they would have hidden it. They are right in this much —that their own ingenuity is a faithful representative of that of the mass; but when the cunning of the individual felon is diverse in character from their own, the felon foils them, of course. This always happens when it is above their own, and very usually when it is below. They have no variation of principle in their investigations; at best, when urged by some unusual emergency —by some extraordinary reward—they extend or exaggerate their old modes of practice, without touching their principles. What, for example, in this case of D—, has been done to vary the principle of action? What is all this boring, and probing, and sounding, and scrutinizing with the microscope, and dividing the surface of the building into registered square inches —what is it all but an exaggeration of the application of the one principle or set of principles of search, which are based upon the one set of notions regarding human ingenuity, to which the Prefect, in the long routine of his duty, has been accustomed? Do you not see he has taken it for granted that all men proceed to conceal a letter, —not exactly in a gimlet-hole bored in a chair-leg — but, at least, in some hole or corner suggested by the same tenor of thought which would urge a man to secrete a letter in a gimlet-hole bored in a chair-leg? And do you not see also, that such recherches nooks for concealment are adapted only for ordinary occasions, and would be adopted only by ordinary intellects; for, in all cases of concealment, a disposal of the article concealed —a disposal of it in this recherche manner, —is, in the very first instance, presumable and presumed; and thus its discovery depends, not at all upon the acumen, but altogether upon the mere care, patience, and determination of the seekers; and where the case is of importance — or, what amounts to the same thing in the policial eyes, when the reward is of magnitude, —the qualities in question have never been known to fail. You will now understand what I meant in suggesting that, had the purloined letter been hidden anywhere within the limits of the Prefect's examination —in other words, had the principle of its concealment been comprehended within the principles of the Prefect —its discovery would have been a matter altogether beyond question. This functionary, however, has been thoroughly mystified; and the remote source of his defeat lies in the supposition that the Minister is a fool, because he has acquired renown as a poet. All fools are poets; this the Prefect feels; and he is merely guilty of a non distributio medii in thence inferring that all poets are fools."

"But is this really the poet?" I asked. "There are two brothers, I know; and both have attained reputation in letters. The Minister I believe has written learnedly on the Differential Calculus. He is a mathematician, and no poet."

"You are mistaken; I know him well; he is both. As poet and mathematician, he would reason well; as mere mathematician, he could not have reasoned at all, and thus would have been at the mercy of the Prefect."

"You surprise me," I said, "by these opinions, which have been contradicted by the voice of the world. You do not mean to set at naught the well-digested idea of centuries. The mathematical reason has long been regarded as the reason par excellence."

"Il y a a parier," replied Dupin, quoting from Chamfort, "'que toute idee publique, toute convention recue, est une sottise, car elle a convenu au plus grand nombre.' The mathematicians, I grant you, have done their best to promulgate the popular error to which you allude, and which is none the less an error for its promulgation as truth. With an art worthy a better cause, for example, they have insinuated the term 'analysis' into application to algebra. The French are the originators of this particular deception; but if a term is of any importance —if words derive any value from applicability —then 'analysis' conveys 'algebra' about as much as, in Latin 'ambitus' implies 'ambition' 'religio' 'religion' or 'homines honesti' a set of honorable men."

"You have a quarrel on hand, I see," said I, "with some of the algebraists of Paris; but proceed."

"I dispute the availability, and thus the value, of that reason which is cultivated in any especial form other than the abstractly logical. I dispute, in particular, the reason educed by mathematical study. The mathematics are the science of form and quantity; mathematical reasoning is merely logic applied to observation upon form and quantity. The great error lies in supposing that even the truths of what is called pure algebra, are abstract or general truths. And this error is so egregious that I am confounded at the universality with which it has been received. Mathematical axioms are not axioms of general truth. What is true of relation —of form and quantity —is often grossly false in regard to morals, for example. In this latter science it is very usually untrue that the aggregated parts are equal to the whole. In chemistry also the axiom fails. In the consideration of motive it fails; for two motives, each of a given value, have not, necessarily, a value when united, equal to the sum of their values apart. There are numerous other mathematical truths which are only truths within the limits of relation. But the mathematician argues, from his finite truths, through habit, as if they were of an absolutely general applicability —as the world indeed imagines them to be. Bryant, in his very learned 'Mythology,' mentions an analogous source of error, when he says that 'although the Pagan fables are not believed, yet we forget ourselves continually, and make inferences from them as existing realities.' With the algebraists, however, who are Pagans themselves, the 'Pagan fables' are believed, and the inferences are made, not so much through lapse of memory, as through an unaccountable addling of the brains. In short, I never yet encountered the mere mathematician who could be trusted out of equal roots, or one who did not clandestinely hold it as a point of his faith that x squared + px was absolutely and unconditionally equal to q. Say to one of these gentlemen, by way of experiment, if you please, that you believe occasions may occur where x squared + px is not altogether equal to q, and, having made him understand what you mean, get out of his reach as speedily as convenient, for, beyond doubt, he will endeavor to knock you down.

"I mean to say," continued Dupin, while I merely laughed at his last observations, "that if the Minister had been no more than a mathematician, the Prefect would have been under no necessity of giving me this check. I knew him, however, as both mathematician and poet, and my measures were adapted to his capacity, with reference to the circumstances by which he was surrounded. I knew him as a courtier, too, and as a bold intriguant. Such a man, I considered, could not fail to be aware of the ordinary policial modes of action. He could not have failed to anticipate —and events have proved that he did not fail to anticipate —the waylayings to which he was subjected. He must have foreseen, I reflected, the secret investigations of his premises. His frequent absences from home at night, which were hailed by the Prefect as certain aids to his success, I regarded only as ruses, to afford opportunity for thorough search to the police, and thus the sooner to impress them with the conviction to which G—, in fact, did finally arrive —the conviction that the letter was not upon the premises. I felt, also, that the whole train of thought, which I was at some pains in detailing to you just now, concerning the invariable principle of policial action in searches for articles concealed —I felt that this whole train of thought would necessarily pass through the mind of the Minister. It would imperatively lead him to despise all the ordinary nooks of concealment. He could not, I reflected, be so weak as not to see that the most intricate and remote recess of his hotel would be as open as his commonest closets to the eyes, to the probes, to the gimlets, and to the microscopes of the Prefect. I saw, in fine, that he would be driven, as a matter of course, to simplicity, if not deliberately induced to it as a matter of choice. You will remember, perhaps, how desperately the Prefect laughed when I suggested, upon our first interview, that it was just possible this mystery troubled him so much on account of its being so very self-evident."

"Yes," said I, "I remember his merriment well. I really thought he would have fallen into convulsions."

"The material world," continued Dupin, "abounds with very

strict analogies to the immaterial; and thus some color of truth has been given to the rhetorical dogma, that metaphor, or simile, may be made to strengthen an argument, as well as to embellish a description. The principle of the vis inertiae, for example, seems to be identical in physics and metaphysics. It is not more true in the former, that a large body is with more difficulty set in motion than a smaller one, and that its subsequent momentum is commensurate with this difficulty, than it is, in the latter, that intellects of the vaster capacity, while more forcible, more constant, and more eventful in their movements than those of inferior grade, are yet the less readily moved, and more embarrassed and full of hesitation in the first few steps of their progress. Again: have you ever noticed which of the street signs, over the shop doors, are the most attractive of attention?"

"I have never given the matter a thought," I said.

"There is a game of puzzles," he resumed, "which is played upon a map. One party playing requires another to find a given word —the name of town, river, state or empire —any word, in short, upon the motley and perplexed surface of the chart. A novice in the game generally seeks to embarrass his opponents by giving them the most minutely lettered names; but the adept selects such words as stretch, in large characters, from one end of the chart to the other. These, like the over-largely lettered signs and placards of the street, escape observation by dint of being excessively obvious; and here the physical oversight is precisely analogous with the moral inapprehension by which the intellect suffers to pass unnoticed those considerations which are too obtrusively and too palpably self-evident. But this is a point, it appears, somewhat above or beneath the understanding of the Prefect. He never once thought it probable, or possible, that the Minister had deposited the letter immediately beneath the nose of the whole world, by way of best preventing any portion of that world from perceiving it.

"But the more I reflected upon the daring, dashing, and discriminating ingenuity of D—; upon the fact that the document must always have been at hand, if he intended to use it to good purpose; and upon the decisive evidence, obtained by the Prefect, that it was not hidden within the limits of that dignitary's ordinary search —the more satisfied I became that, to conceal this letter, the Minister had resorted to the comprehensive and sagacious expedient of not attempting to conceal it at all.

"Full of these ideas, I prepared myself with a pair of green spectacles, and called one fine morning, quite by accident, at the Ministerial hotel. I found D—at home, yawning, lounging, and dawdling, as usual, and pretending to be in the last extremity of ennui. He is, perhaps, the most really energetic human being now alive —but that is only when nobody sees him.

"To be even with him, I complained of my weak eyes, and lamented the necessity of the spectacles, under cover of which I cautiously and thoroughly surveyed the apartment, while seemingly intent only upon the conversation of my host.

"I paid special attention to a large writing-table near which he sat, and upon which lay confusedly, some miscellaneous letters and other papers, with one or two musical instruments and a few books. Here, however, after a long and very deliberate scrutiny, I saw nothing to excite particular suspicion.

"At length my eyes, in going the circuit of the room, fell upon a trumpery filigree card-rack of pasteboard, that hung dangling by a dirty blue ribbon, from a little brass knob just beneath the middle of the mantelpiece. In this rack, which had three or four compartments, were five or six visiting cards and a solitary letter. This last was much soiled and crumpled. It was torn nearly in two, across the middle —as if a design, in the first instance, to tear it entirely up as worthless, had been altered, or stayed, in the second. It had a large black seal, bearing the D—cipher very conspicuously, and was addressed, in a diminutive female hand, to D—, the minister, himself. It was thrust carelessly, and even, as it seemed, contemptuously, into one of the upper divisions of the rack.

"No sooner had I glanced at this letter, than I concluded it to be that of which I was in search. To be sure, it was, to all appearance, radically different from the one of which the Prefect had read us so minute a description. Here the seal was large and black, with the D—cipher; there it was small and red, with the ducal arms of the S—family. Here, the address, to the Minister, was diminutive and feminine; there the superscription, to a certain royal personage, was markedly bold and decided; the size alone formed a point of correspondence. But, then, the radicalness of these differences, which was excessive; the dirt; the soiled and torn condition of the paper, so inconsistent with the true methodical habits of D—, and so suggestive of a design to delude the beholder into an idea of the worthlessness of the document; these things, together with the hyperobtrusive situation of this document, full in the view of every visitor, and thus exactly in accordance with the conclusions to which I had previously arrived; these things, I say, were strongly corroborative of suspicion, in one who came with the intention to suspect.

"I protracted my visit as long as possible, and, while I maintained a most animated discussion with the Minister, on a topic which I knew well had never failed to interest and excite him, I kept my attention really riveted upon the letter. In this examination, I committed to memory its external appearance and arrangement in the rack; and also fell, at length, upon a discovery which set at rest whatever trivial doubt I might have entertained. In scrutinizing the edges of the paper, I observed them to be more chafed than seemed necessary. They presented the broken appearance which is manifested when a stiff paper, having been once folded and pressed with a folder, is refolded in a reversed direction, in the same creases or edges which had formed the original fold. This discovery was sufficient. It was clear to me that the letter had been turned, as a glove, inside out, re-directed, and re-sealed. I bade the Minister good morning, and took my departure at once, leaving a gold snuff-box upon the table.

"The next morning I called for the snuff-box, when we resumed, quite eagerly, the conversation of the preceding day. While thus engaged, however, a loud report, as if of a pistol, was heard immediately beneath the windows of the hotel, and was succeeded by a series of fearful screams, and the shoutings of a mob. D— rushed to a casement, threw it open, and looked out. In the meantime, I stepped to the card-rack, took the letter, put it in my pocket, and replaced it by a fac-simile, (so far as regards externals,) which I had carefully prepared at my lodgings; imitating the D—cipher, very readily, by means of a seal formed of bread.

"The disturbance in the street had been occasioned by the frantic behavior of a man with a musket. He had fired it among a crowd of women and children. It proved, however, to have been without ball, and the fellow was suffered to go his way as a lunatic or a drunkard. When he had gone, D-came from the window, whither I had followed him immediately upon securing the object in view. Soon afterwards I bade him farewell. The pretended lunatic was a man in my own pay."

"But what purpose had you," I asked, "in replacing the letter by a fac-simile? Would it not have been better, at the first visit, to have seized it openly, and departed?"

"D—," replied Dupin, "is a desperate man, and a man of nerve. His hotel, too, is not without attendants devoted to his interests. Had I made the wild attempt you suggest, I might never have left the Ministerial presence alive. The good people of Paris might have heard of me no more. But I had an object apart from these considerations. You know my political prepossessions. In this matter, I act as a partisan of the lady concerned. For eighteen months the Minister has had her in his power. She has now him in hers; since, being unaware that the letter is not in his possession, he will proceed with his exactions as if it was. Thus will he inevitably commit himself, at once, to his political destruction. His downfall, too, will not be more precipitate than awkward. It is all very well to talk about the facilis descensus Averni; but in all kinds of climbing, as Catalani said of singing, it is far more easy to get up than to come down. In the present instance I have no sympathy —at least no pity —for him who descends. He is the monstrum horrendum, an unprincipled man of genius. I confess, however, that I should like very well to know the precise character of his thoughts, when, being defied by her whom the Prefect terms 'a certain personage,' he is reduced to opening the letter which I left for him in the card-rack."

"How? Did you put any thing particular in it?"

"Why —it did not seem altogether right to leave the interior blank —that would have been insulting. D—, at Vienna once, did me an evil turn, which I told him, quite good-humoredly, that I should remember. So, as I knew he would feel some curiosity in regard to the identity of the person who had outwitted him, I thought it a pity not to give him a clue. He is well acquainted with my MS., and I just copied into the middle of the blank sheet the words—

—Un dessein si funeste,

S'il n'est digne d'Atree, est digne de Thyeste.

They are to be found in Crebillon's 'Atree.'"

THE END

II

Sherwood Anderson

2.1 The Introductory Remarks of Sherwood Anderson

Sherwood Anderson (1876—1941) is a noteworthy American modernist writer. He first introduces Freud's psychological theoretical viewpoint to his literary writings. He is good at depicting his characters' attaining enlightenment from something or some occasion in a sudden way in a story. Many American modern writers derive nourishment from his literary writings. In some sense he is the father of the American modern writers. Sherwood Anderson was born in a small town, Ohio. As a son of a manual laborer, he could not acquire his formal schooling. To help his father support his family, he left his hometown for Chicago and worked in a factory. Such experience provided the vivid materials for his later writings. In 1898, Anderson enlisted the Army, one year later he returned to his hometown and studied at a university for one year, and then he went to Chicago again where he wrote advertisements for an advertisement firm to earn his living. Not long after he rose as a rich businessman. Yet he often felt worried because he disliked such meaningless life and he wanted to seek for the essence of life. So he made his choice: quitted his position as a wealthy boss and concentrated on his literary writings. In 1916, Anderson published his first novel *Windy McPherson's Son Settled in a Small Town*, which centered on the theme of American dream. However, *Winesburg Ohio* brought him the fame. This collection of stories recorded the puzzle of the peasants' life and their desire and expectation of freedom, love and happiness, and also portrayed many lovely deformed characters. After the publication of *Winesburg Ohio*, Sherwood Anderson completed his next novel for *Poor White* in 1920 and criticized the destruction made by modern industrial development. Anderson published three collections of short stories, *The Triumph of the Egg*, *Horses and Men* and *Death in the Woods* and other stories. In addition to the novel and stories, Sherwood Anderson also created his other celebrated works such as *A Story-Teller's Story*, *I Want to Know Why* and *Sherwood Anderson's Memoirs*, etc.

Sherwood Anderson interprets his theme in his writings: his adherence to the peaceful and harmonious life in the good old days in the small town. He reveals his detest of modern industrial civilization and depicts his understanding for the young generation's life. Anderson's writing style is similar to that used by Mark Twain in his many generations of writers at present.

2.2 Comment on *The Egg*

Sherwood Anderson is viewed as "the father of American writers" because he adheres to American traditional style, absorbing in the writing technique in *the Bible*, borrowing the simple colloquial way from Mark Twain's short stories and mixing them with his own life experience as well as his good understanding of the life in american mid-west small town to create a lot of excellent short stories with profound connotation.

The short story *The Egg* is one of Anderson's best-known stories. It is selected from *The Triumph of The Egg*, one of Anderson's famous collections of short stories (1921), based on his experience from his childhood in his father's farm. The story is set in a small town of Winesburg in Ohio. In this story Anderson presents his theme of loneliness, dissimilation and epiphany. From a unique respective, Anderson depicts the peaceful life and natural beauty there before the modern industrialization and reveals his disgust of modern industrialization. The author employs the first person point of view to lead the story. The protagonist "I" is a small boy who narrates the story that happened in his father's farm. To get up like other Americans, the boy's parents don't have an idea that something tragic can happen to chickens. Many chickens get diseases such as cholera, pip and other diseases. Finally they all die. The boy's father and mother have worked hard in their chicken farm for ten years, but they can not make any profit from their chicken-raising cause. Their hope for making money from chickens is disillusioned. The boy's family starts out their journey through life for town of Bidwell. In the town, the boy's parents open a restaurant to realize their American dream. To entertain the young customers, the family tries to make smiles instead of their glum looks. The boy's father often shows what he can do by means of eggshell kept in a wire basket on the counter. However, "An egg ruins his new impulse in life," he wants to establish his reputation to attack his guests through making eggshell do the tricks. One evening, he makes his egg tricks for his only guest Joe kane. He tries his best to do but fails. Joe Kane neglects his tricks and reads his newspaper. Irritated by his misfortune, the boy's father throws an egg to his guest and then begins to cry.

2.3 The Text of *The Egg*

MY FATHER was, I am sure, intended by nature to be a cheerful, kindly man. Until he was thirty-four years old he worked as a farmhand for a man named Thomas Butterworth whose place lay near the town of Bidwell, Ohio. He had then a horse of his own and on Saturday evenings drove into town to spend a few hours in social intercourse with other farmhands. In town he drank several glasses of beer and stood about in Ben Head's saloon—crowded on Saturday evenings with visiting farmhands. Songs were sung and glasses thumped on the bar. At ten o' clock father drove home along a lonely country road, made his horse comfortable for the night and himself went to bed, quite happy in his position in life. He had at that time no notion of trying to rise in the world.

It was in the spring of his thirty-fifth year that father married my mother, then a country schoolteacher, and in the following spring I came wriggling and crying into the world. Something happened to the two people. They became ambitious. The American passion for getting up in the world took possession of them.

It may have been that mother was responsible. Being a schoolteacher she had no doubt read books and magazines. She had, I presume, read of how Garfield, Lincoln, and other Americans rose from poverty to fame and greatness and as I lay beside her—in the days of her lying-in—she may have dreamed that I would someday rule men and cities. At any rate she induced father to give up his place as a farmhand, sell his horse and embark on an independent enterprise of his own. She was a tall silent woman with a long nose and troubled grey eyes. For herself she wanted nothing. For father and me she was incurably ambitious.

The first venture into which the two people went turned out badly. They rented ten acres of poor stony land on Griggs's Road, eight miles from Bidwell, and launched into chicken raising. I grew into boyhood on the place and got my first impressions of life there. From the beginning they were impressions of disaster and if, in my turn, I am a gloomy man inclined to see the darker side of life, I attribute it to the fact that what should have been for me the happy joyous days of childhood were spent on a chicken farm.

One unversed in such matters can have no notion of the many and tragic things that can happen to a chicken. It is born out of an egg, lives for a few weeks as a tiny fluffy thing such as you will see pictured on Easter cards, then becomes hideously naked, eats quantities of corn and meal bought by the sweat of your father's brow, gets diseases called pip, cholera, and other names, stands looking with stupid eyes at the sun, becomes sick and dies. A few hens and now and then a rooster intended to serve God's mysterious ends, struggle through to maturity. The hens lay eggs out of which come other chickens and the dreadful cycle is thus made complete. It is all unbelievably complex. Most philosophers must have been raised on chicken farms. One hopes for so much from a chicken and is so dreadfully disillusioned. Small chickens, just setting out on the journey of life, look so bright and alert and they are in fact so dreadfully stupid. They are so much like people they mix one up in one's judgments of life. If disease does not kill them they wait until your expectations are thoroughly aroused and then walk under the wheels of a wagon—to go squashed and dead back to their maker. Vermin infest their youth, and fortunes must be spent for curative powders. In later life I have seen how a literature has been built up on the subject of fortunes to be made out of the raising of chickens. It is intended to be read by the gods who have just eaten of the tree of the knowledge of good and evil. It is a hopeful literature and declares that much may be done by simple ambitious people who own a few hens. Do not be led astray by it. It was not written for you. Go hunt for gold on the frozen hills of Alaska, put your faith in the honesty of a politician, believe if you will that the world is daily growing better and that good will triumph over evil, but do not read and believe the literature that is written concerning the hen. It was not written for you.

I, however, digress. My tale does not primarily concern itself with the hen. If correctly told it will center on the egg. For ten years my father and mother struggled to make our chicken farm pay and then they gave up that struggle and began another. They moved into the town of Bidwell, Ohio and embarked in the restaurant business. After ten years of worry with incubators that did not hatch, and with tiny—and in their own way lovely—balls of fluff that passed on into semi-naked pullerhood and from that into dead henhood, we threw all aside and packed our belongings on a wagon driving down Griggs's Road toward Bidwell, a tiny caravan of hope looking for a new place from which to start on our upward journey through life.

We must have been a sad looking lot, not, I fancy, unlike refugees fleeing from a battlefield. Mother and I walked in the road. The wagon that contained our goods had been borrowed for the day from Mr. Albert Griggs, a neighbor. Out of its sides stuck the legs of cheap chairs and at the back of the pile of beds, tables, and boxes filled with kitchen utensils was a crate of live chickens, and on top of that the baby carriage in which I had been wheeled about in my infancy. Why we stuck to the baby carriage I don't know. It was unlikely other children would be born and the wheels were broken. People who have few possessions cling tightly to those they have. That is one of the facts that make life so discouraging.

Father rode on top of the wagon. He was then a bald-headed man of forty-five, a little fat and from long association with mother and the chickens he had become habitually silent and discouraged. All during our ten years on the chicken farm he had worked as a laborer on neighboring farms and most of the money he had earned had been spent for remedies to cure chicken diseases, on Wilmer's White Wonder Cholera Cure or Professor Bidlow's Egg Producer or some other preparations that mother found advertised in the poultry papers. There were two little patches of hair on father's head just a-bove his ears. I remember that as a child I used to sit looking at him when he had gone to sleep in a chair before the stove on Sunday afternoons in the winter. I had at that rime already begun to read books and have notions of my own and the bald path that led over the top of his head was, I fancied, something like a broad road, such a road as Caesar might have made on which to lead his legions out of Rome and into the wonders of an unknown world. The tufts of hair that grew above father's ears were, I thought, like forests. I fell into a half-sleeping, half-waking state and dreamed I was a tiny thing going along the road into a far beautiful place where there were no chicken farms and where life was a happy eggless affair.

One might write a book concerning our flight from the chicken farm into town. Mother and I walked the entire eight miles—she to be sure that nothing fell from the wagon and I to see the wonders of the world. On the seat of the wagon beside father was his greatest treasure. I will tell you of that.

On a chicken farm where hundreds and even thousands of chickens come out of eggs, surprising things sometimes happen. Grotesques are born out of eggs as out of people. The accident does not often occur—perhaps once in a thousand births. A chicken is, you see, born that has four legs, two pairs of wings, two heads or what not. The things do not live. They go quickly back to the hand of their maker that has for a moment trembled. The fact that the poor little things could not live was one of the tragedies of life to father. He had some sort of notion that if he could but bring into henhood or roosterhood a five-legged hen or a two-headed rooster his fortune would be made. He dreamed of taking the wonder about to county fairs and of growing rich by exhibiting it to other farmhands.

At any rate he saved all the little monstrous things that had been born on our chicken farm. They were preserved in alcohol and put each in its own glass bottle. These he had carefully put into a box and on our journey into town it was carried on the wagon seat beside him. He drove the horses with one hand and with the other clung to the box. When we got to our destination the box was taken down at once and the bottles removed. All during our days as keepers of a restaurant in the town of Bidwell, Ohio, the grotesques in their little glass bottles sat on a shelf back of the counter. Mother sometimes protested but father was a rock on the subject of his treasure. The grotesques were, he declared, valuable. People, he said, liked to look at strange and wonderful things.

Did I say that we embarked in the restaurant business in the town of Bidwell, Ohio? I exaggerated a little. The town itself lay at the foot of a low hill and on the shore of a small river. The railroad did not run through the town and the station was a mile away to the north at a place called Pickleville. There had been a cider mill and pickle factory at the station, but before the time of our coming they had both gone out of business. In the morning and in the evening busses came down to the station along a road called Turner's Pike from the hotel on the main street of Bidwell. Our going to the out-of-the-way place to embark in the restaurant business was mother's idea. She talked of it for a year and then one day went off and rented an empty store building opposite the railroad station. It was her idea that the restaurant would be profitable. Travelling men, she said, would be always waiting around to take trains out of town and town people would come to the station to await incoming trains. They would come to the restaurant to buy pieces of pie and drink coffee. Now that I am older I know that she had another motive in going. She was ambitious for me. She wanted me to rise in the world, to get into a town school and become a man of the towns.

At Pickleville father and mother worked hard as they always had done. At first there was the necessity of putting our place into shape to be a restaurant. That took a month. Father built a shelf on which he put tins of vegetables. He painted a sign on which he put his name in large red letters. Below his name was the sharp command—"EAT HERE"—that was so seldom obeyed. A showcase was bought and filled with cigars and tobacco. Mother scrubbed the floor and the walls of the room. I went to school in the town and was glad to be away from the farm and from the presence of the discouraged, sad-looking chickens. Still I was not very joyous. In the evening I walked home from school along Turner's Pike and remembered the children I had seen playing in the town school yard. A troop of little girls had gone hopping about and singing. I tried that. Down along the frozen road I went hopping solemnly on one leg. "Hippity hop to the barber shop," I sang shrilly. Then I stopped and looked doubtfully about. I was afraid of being seen in my gay mood. It must have seemed to me that I was doing a thing that should not be done by one who, like myself, had been raised on a chicken farm where death was a daily visitor.

Mother decided that our restaurant should remain open at night. At ten in the evening a passenger train went north past our door followed by a local freight. The freight crew had switching to do in Pickleville and when the work was done they came to our restaurant for hot coffee and food. Sometimes one of them ordered a fried egg. In the morning at four they returned northbound and again visited us. A little trade began to grow up. Mother slept at night and during the day tended the restaurant and fed our boarders while father slept. He slept in the same bed mother had occupied during the night and I went off to the town of Bidwell and to school. During the long nights, while mother and I slept, father cooked meats that were to go into sandwiches for the lunch baskets of our boarders. Then an idea in regard to getting up in the world came into his head. The American spirit took hold of him. He also became ambitious.

In the long nights when there was little to do father had time to think. That was his undoing. He decided that he had in the past been an unsuccessful man because he had not been cheerful enough and that in the future he would adopt a cheerful outlook on life. In the early morning he came upstairs and got into bed with mother. She woke and the two talked. From my bed in the corner I listened.

It was father's idea that both he and mother should try to entertain the people who came to eat at our restaurant. I cannot now remember his words, but he gave the impression of one about to become in some obscure way a kind of public entertainer. When people, particularly young people from the town of Bidwell, came into our place, as on very rare occasions they did, bright entertaining conversation was to be made. From father's words I gathered that something of the jolly innkeeper effect was to be sought. Mother must have been doubtful from the first, but she said nothing discouraging. It was father's notion that a passion for the company of himself and mother would spring up in the breasts of the younger people of the town of Bidwell. In the evening bright happy groups would come singing down Turner's Pike. They would troop shouting with joy and laughter into our place. There would be song and festivity. I do not mean to give the impression that father spoke so elaborately of the matter. He was as I have said an uncommunicative man. "They want some place to go. I tell you they want some place to go," he said over and over. That was as far as he got. My own imagination has filled in the blanks.

For two or three weeks this notion of father's invaded our house. We did not talk much but in our daily lives tried earnestly to make smiles take the place of glum looks. Mother smiled at the boarders and I, catching the infection, smiled at our cat. Father became a little feverish in his anxiety to please. There was no doubt lurking somewhere in him a touch of the spirit of the showman. He did not waste much of his ammunition on the railroad men he served at night but seemed to be waiting for a young man or woman from Bidwell to come in to show what he could do. On the counter in the restaurant there was a wire basket kept always filled with eggs, and it must have been before his eyes when the idea of being entertaining was born in his brain. There was something pre-natal about the way eggs kept themselves connected with the development of his idea. At any rate an egg ruined his new impulse in life. Late one night I was awakened by a roar of anger coming from father's throat. Both mother and I sat upright in our beds. With trembling hands she lighted a lamp that stood on a table by her head. Downstairs the front door of our restaurant went shut with a bang and in a few minutes father tramped up the stairs. He held an egg in his hand and his hand trembled as though he were having a chill. There was a half insane light in his eyes. As he stood glaring at us I was sure he intended throwing the egg at either mother or me. Then he laid it gently on the table beside the lamp and dropped on his knees beside mother's bed. He began to cry like a boy and I, carried away by his grief, cried with him. The two of us filled the little upstairs room with our wailing voices. It is ridiculous, but of the picture we made I can remember only the fact that mother's hand continually stroked the bald path that ran across the top of his head. I have forgotten what mother said to him and how she induced him to tell her of what had happened downstairs. His explanation also has gone out of my mind. I remember only my own grief and fright and the shiny path over father's head glowing in the lamplight as he knelt by the bed.

As to what happened downstairs. For some unexplainable reason I know the story as well as though I had been a witness to my father's discomfiture. One in time gets to know many unexplainable things. On that evening young Joe Kane, son of a merchant of Bidwell, came to Pickleville to meet his father, who was expected on the ten o'clock evening train from the south. The train was three hours late and Joe came into our place to loaf about and to wait for its arrival. The local freight train came in and the freight crew was fed. Joe was left alone in the restaurant with father.

From the moment he came into our place the Bidwell young man must have been puzzled by my father's actions. It was his notion that father was angry at him for hanging around. He noticed that the restaurant keeper was apparently disturbed by his presence and he thought of going out. However, it began to rain and he did not fancy the long walk to town and back. He bought a five-cent cigar and ordered a cup of coffee. He had a newspaper in his pocket and took it out and began to read. "I'm waiting for the evening train. It's late," he said apologetically.

For a long time, father, whom Joe Kane had never seen before, remained silently gazing at his visitor. He was no doubt suffering from an attack of stage fright. As so often happens in life he had thought so much and so often of the situation that now confronted him that he was somewhat nervous in its presence.

For one thing, he did not know what to do with his hands. He thrust one of them nervously over the counter and shook hands with Joe Kane. "How-de-do," he said. Joe Kane put his newspaper down and stared at him. Father's eye lighted on the basket of eggs that sat on the counter and he began to talk. "Well," he began hesitatingly, "well, you have heard of Christopher Columbus, eh?" He seemed to be angry. "That Christopher Columbus was a cheat," he declared emphatically. "He talked of making an egg stand on its end. He talked, he did, and then he went and broke the end of the egg."

My father seemed to his visitor to be beside himself at the duplicity of Christopher Columbus. He muttered and swore. He declared it was wrong to teach children that Christopher Columbus was a great man when, after all, he cheated at the critical moment. He had declared he would make an egg stand on end and then when his bluff had been called he had done a trick. Still grumbling at Columbus, father took an egg from the basket on the counter and began to walk up and down. He rolled the egg between the palms of his hands. He smiled genially. He began to mumble words regarding the effect to be produced on an egg by the electricity that comes out of the human body. He declared that without breaking its shell and by virtue of rolling it back and forth in his hands he could stand the egg on its end. He explained that the warmth of his hands and the gentle rolling movement he gave the egg created a new center of gravity, and Joe Kane was mildly interested. "I have handled thousands of eggs," father said. "No one knows more about eggs than I do."

He stood the egg on the counter and it fell on its side. He tried the trick again and again, each time rolling the egg between the palms of his hands and saying the words regarding the wonders of electricity and the laws of gravity. When after a half hour's effort he did succeed in making the egg stand for a moment, he looked up to find that his visitor was no longer watching. By the time he had succeeded in calling Joe Kane's attention to the success of his effort, the egg had again rolled over and lay on its side.

Afire with the showman's passion and at the same time a good deal disconcerted by the failure of his first effort, father now took the bottles containing the poultry monstrosities down from their place on the shelf and began to show them to his visitor. "How would you like to have seven legs and two heads like this fellow?" he asked, exhibiting the most remarkable of his treasures. A cheerful smile played over his face. He reached over the counter and tried to slap Joe Kane on the shoulder as he had seen men do in Ben Head's saloon when he was a young farmhand and drove to town on Saturday evenings. His visitor was made a little ill by the sight of the body of the terribly deformed bird floating in the alcohol in the bottle and got up to go. Coming from behind the counter, father took hold of the young man's arm and led him back to his seat. He grew a little angry and for a moment had to turn his face away and force himself to smile. Then he put the bottles back on the shelf. In an outburst of generosity he fairly compelled Joe Kane to have a fresh cup of coffee and another cigar at his expense. Then he took a pan and filling it with vinegar, taken from a jug that sat beneath the counter, he declared himself about to do a new trick. "I will heat this egg in this pan of vinegar," he said. "Then I will put it through the neck of a bottle without breaking the shell. When the egg is inside the bottle it will resume its normal shape and the shell will become hard again. Then I will give the bottle with the egg in it to you. You can take it about with you wherever you go. People will want to know how you got the egg in the bottle. Don't tell them. Keep them guessing. That is the way to have fun with this trick."

Father grinned and winked at his visitor. Joe Kane decided that the man who confronted him was mildly insane but harmless. He drank the cup of coffee that had been given him and began to read his paper again. When the egg had been heated in vinegar, father carried it on a spoon to the counter and going into a back room got an empty bottle. He was angry because his visitor did not watch him as he began to do his trick, but nevertheless went cheerfully to work. For a long time he struggled, trying to get the egg to go through the neck of the bottle. He put the pan of vinegar back on the stove, intending to reheat the egg, then picked it up and burned his fingers. After a second bath in the hot vinegar, the shell of the egg had been softened a little but not enough for his purpose. He worked and worked and a spirit of desperate determination took possession of him. When he thought that at last the trick was about to be consummated, the delayed train came in at the station and Joe Kane started to go nonchalantly out at the door. Father made a last desperate effort to conquer the egg and make it do the thing that would establish his reputation as one who knew how to entertain guests who came into his restaurant. He worried the egg. He attempted to be somewhat rough with it. He swore and the sweat stood out on his forehead. The egg broke under his hand. When the contents spurted over his clothes, Joe Kane, who had stopped at the door, turned and laughed.

A roar of anger rose from my father's throat. He danced and shouted a string of inarticulate words. Grabbing another egg from the basket on the counter, he threw it, just missing the head of the young man as he dodged through the door and escaped.

Father came upstairs to mother and me with an egg in his hand. I do not know what he intended to do. I imagine he had some idea of destroying it, of destroying all eggs, and that he intended to let mother and me see him begin. When, however, he got into the presence of mother something happened to him. He laid the egg gently on the table and dropped on his knees by the bed as I have already explained. He later decided to close the restaurant for the night and to come upstairs and get into bed. When he did so he blew out the light and after much muttered conversation both he and mother went to sleep. I suppose I went to sleep also, but my sleep was troubled. I awoke at dawn and for a long time looked at the egg that lay on the table. I wondered why eggs had to be and why from the egg came the hen who again laid the egg. The question got into my blood. It has stayed there, I imagine, because I am the son of my father. At any rate, the problem remains unsolved in my mind. And that, I conclude, is but another evidence of the complete and final triumph of the egg—at least as far as my family is concerned.

III

Eugene O' Neill

3.1 The Introductory Remarks of Eugene O' Neill

In some sense, Eugene O' Neill (1888—1953) explores a new way for real American play writing. His popularity in the play circle of world is due to his plays which demonstrate American style and his unique tragic theme. He devotes his life to cause of American play acting, performing and writing, penning a lot of celebrated works. O' Neill seems to try expressing his contemplation of human life and his exploration of humanity through his observation of American society. He experiments a variety of writing techniques and different dramatic forms such as expressionism, symbolism and realism. From his posthumous autobiographical masterpiece *Long Day's Journey into Night*, O' Neill portrays the dilemma of the American people in his time and struggles to free-themselves through his own experiments with psychological expressionism.

Eugene O' Neill was born in an actor's family in New York City in 1888. His father, James O' Neill earned his living by joining a company to make constant travel acting. So his family spent several years "just drifting." O' Neill attended Princeton for one year and he was sent away from Princeton because of his rebellious lifestyle and drinking, and then he worked for a newspaper as a reporter for a short time. He determined to join in his father's company and try acting. The turning point in O' Neill life is that he was infected with tuberculosis in 1912, a deadly illness, which makes him begin to think about what kind of way of life he should start. At the same time he can take advantage of his time to remain idle to read Greek tragic poets, Ibsen, Strindberg and other famous dramatists' works, and lay a good foundation for his later play writings. O' Neill was taken in Harvard for one term as a special student in Gorge Baker's 47 workshops. He tries writing his first dramatic book, *Thirst: And Other One Act plays* soon makes it in white and black. *Beyond the Horizon* (1920) is his famous play which brought him fame. In this play, O' Neill tries to interpret his profound understanding of the issue: the choice of one's life way. He was afforded the Pulitzer Prize for it. In 1921, O' Neill produced his other famous play *Anna Christie*, which rendered him with the Pulitzer Prize for the second time. Following this play was *The Hairy Ape*, a famous expressional play. It and O' Neill's another expressional play *The Emperor Jones* (1920) reflect O' Neill's philosophical point of view and his seek for humans' psychological state in modern society. *Desire Under the Elms* (1924) became a television staple. In his later years,

O' Neill suffered with various illness, but he still insisted on writing. His best works are written during this period, such as *The Iceman Cometh* (1939), *Long Day's Journey into Night* (1941) and *A Noon for the Misbegotten*, etc.

Eugene O' Neill is regarded as an independent modern dramatist in America. His wide reading provides him with material force to dramatize the existential condition of modern people in modern society, to unfold the various conflicts between man and man, between man and himself. His great achievements of playwriting is also built on his artistic touch and devices of his stage management.

3.2 Comment on *The Hairy Ape*

Eugene O' Neill's *The Hairy Ape* is one of the most typical works in his second dramatical writing period. In his first dramatical period, O' Neill adopts realistic writing style to pen his plays and makes great achievement on it. As a mature dramatist, O' Neill tries not only to open up the creative topics of his plays, but also to explore different modern dramatic writing techniques in his writing. He borrows and develops the expressionist writing style initiated by Sweden playwright, August Strindberg combining his own life experience and fate with those of the main protagonists to illustrate his real psychological significance. It's not hard for us to have a good comprehension of O' Neill proposal of his dramatic creation that he intends to discuss the different forces existed in the human nature and presents his protagonists' interior world and their desperate struggle for changing their destinies.

The Hairy Ape is one of O' Neill's famous expressionist plays, which demonstrates his theme: After WWII, modern man lost their sense of belonging and they perceived it difficult for them to find a way to go in their journey of life in human society through the depiction of the protagonist Yanker's life experience. Yanker is a fireman in a ship, who is strong and large but simple-minded. He thought he was "something" important in his working position on his ship. After he has been treated as "a dirty animal" by the upper class people, Yanker comes to recognize his humble social position and pitiful plight as an underdog. Out of desperation, Yanker quits his job, roaming in a zoo, where he takes a notice of an ape seizing the bars of the cage in which he is put. Associated the ape's imprisonment in the cage with his own situation working as a fireman in a narrow space of boiler room on the ship where it is like a prison, Yanker holds so much sympathy for the ape that he helps the ape escape from its cage, enjoying its freedom. Unfortunately, instead of fleeing immediately, the ape attacks Yanker suddenly and pinches Yanker's neck and kills him. From the end of the story, we can see O' Neill consistent theme as well as his contemplation of human nature. Influenced by naturalist doctrine, O' Neill suggests his idea that the survival of the fittest governs nature and human society by a good example of Yanker's striving for his social identity and miserable destiny.

In *The Hairy Ape*, O' Neill makes good use of his symbolic way to interpret his idea. The hairy ape is used to symbolize the men living at the bottom of the society, who are represented by the protagonist, Yanker. The ape's cage and the stoker room represent the prison to which human being are confined.

3.3 The Text of *The Hairy Ape*

Scene II

Section of promenade deck, two days out—morning

SCENE—Two days out. A section of the promenade deck. MILDRED DOUGLAS and her aunt are discovered reclining in deck chairs. The former is a girl of twenty, slender, delicate, with a pale, pretty face marred by a self-conscious expression of disdainful superiority. She looks fretful, nervous and discontented, bored by her own anemia. Her aunt is a pompous and proud—and fat—old lady. She is a type even to the point of a double chin and lorgnettes. She is dressed pretentiously, as if afraid her face alone would never indicate her position in life. MILDRED is dressed all in white.

The impression to be conveyed by this scene is one of the beautiful, vivid life of the sea all about—sunshine on the deck in a great flood, the fresh sea wind blowing across it. In the midst of this, these two incongruous, artificial figures, inert and disharmonious, the elder like a gray lump of dough touched up with rouge, the younger looking as if the vitality of her stock had been sapped before she was conceived, so that she is the expression not of its life energy but merely of the artificialities that energy had won for itself in the spending.

MILDRED—[Looking up with affected dreaminess.] How the

black smoke swirls back against the sky! Is it not beautiful?

AUNT—[Without looking up.] I dislike smoke of any kind.

MILDRED—My great-grandmother smoked a pipe—a clay pipe.

AUNT—[Ruffling.] Vulgar!

MILDRED—She was too distant a relative to be vulgar. Time mellows pipes.

AUNT—[Pretending boredom but irritated.] Did the sociology you took up at college teach you that—to play the ghoul on every possible occasion, excavating old bones? Why not let your great-grandmother rest in her grave?

MILDRED—[Dreamily.] With her pipe beside her—puffing in Paradise.

AUNT—[With spite.] Yes, you are a natural born ghoul. You are even getting to look like one, my dear.

MILDRED—[In a passionless tone.] I detest you, Aunt. [Looking at her critically.] Do you know what you remind me of? Of a cold pork pudding against a background of linoleum tablecloth in the kitchen of a—but the possibilities are wearisome. [She closes her eyes.]

AUNT—[With a bitter laugh.] Merci for your candor. But since I am and must be your chaperone—in appearance, at least—let us patch up some sort of armed truce. For my part you are quite free to indulge any pose of eccentricity that beguiles you—as long as you observe the amenities—

MILDRED—[Drawling.] The inanities?

AUNT—[Going on as if she hadn't heard.] After exhausting

the morbid thrills of social service work on New York's East Side—how they must have hated you, by the way, the poor that you made so much poorer in their own eyes! —you are now bent on making your slumming international. Well, I hope Whitechapel will provide the needed nerve tonic. Do not ask me to chaperone you there, however. I told your father I would not. I loathe deformity. We will hire an army of detectives and you may investigate everything—they allow you to see.

MILDRED—[Protesting with a trace of genuine earnestness.] Please do not mock at my attempts to discover how the other half lives. Give me credit for some sort of groping sincerity in that at least. I would like to help them. I would like to be some use in the world. Is it my fault I don't know how? I would like to be sincere, to touch life somewhere. [With weary bitterness.] But I'm afraid I have neither the vitality nor integrity. All that was burnt out in our stock before I was born. Grandfather's blast furnaces, flaming to the sky, melting steel, making millions—then father keeping those home fires burning, making more millions—and little me at the tail-end of it all. I'm a waste product in the Bessemer process—like the millions. Or rather, I inherit the acquired trait of the by-product, wealth, but none of the energy, none of the strength of the steel that made it. I am sired by gold and damed by it, as they say at the race track—damned in more ways than one. [She laughs mirthlessly.]

AUNT—[Unimpressed—superciliously.] You seem to be going in for sincerity to-day. It isn't becoming to you, really—except as an obvious pose. Be as artificial as you are, I advise. There's a sort of sincerity in that, you know. And, after all, you must confess you like that better.

MILDRED—[Again affected and bored.] Yes, I suppose I do. Pardon me for my outburst. When a leopard complains of its spots, it must sound rather grotesque. [In a mocking tone.] Purr, little leopard. Purr, scratch, tear, kill, gorge yourself and be happy—

only stay in the jungle where your spots are camouflage. In a cage they make you conspicuous.

AUNT—I don't know what you are talking about.

MILDRED—It would be rude to talk about anything to you. Let's just talk. [She looks at her wrist watch.] Well, thank goodness, it's about time for them to come for me. That ought to give me a new thrill, Aunt.

AUNT—[Affectedly troubled.] You don't mean to say you're really going? The dirt—the heat must be frightful—

MILDRED—Grandfather started as a puddler. I should have inherited an immunity to heat that would make a salamander shiver. It will be fun to put it to the test.

AUNT—But don't you have to have the captain's—or someone's—permission to visit the stokehole?

MILDRED—[With a triumphant smile.] I have it—both his and the chief engineer's. Oh, they didn't want to at first, in spite of my social service credentials. They didn't seem a bit anxious that I should investigate how the other half lives and works on a ship. So I had to tell them that my father, the president of Nazareth Steel, chairman of the board of directors of this line, had told me it would be all right.

AUNT—He didn't.

MILDRED—How naive age makes one! But I said he did, Aunt. I even said he had given me a letter to them—which I had lost. And they were afraid to take the chance that I might be lying. [Excitedly.] So it's ho! For the stokehole. The second engineer is to escort me. [Looking at her watch again.] It's time. And here he comes, I think. [The SECOND ENGINEER enters. He is a husky, fine-looking man of thirty-five or so. He stops before the two and tips his cap, visibly embarrassed and ill-at-ease.]

SECOND ENGINEER—Miss Douglas?

MILDRED—Yes. [Throwing off her rugs and getting to her feet.] Are we all ready to start?

SECOND ENGINEER—In just a second, ma'am. I'm waiting for the Fourth. He's coming along.

MILDRED—[With a scornful smile.] You don't care to shoulder this responsibility alone, is that it?

SECOND ENGINEER—[Forcing a smile.] Two are better than one. [Disturbed by her eyes, glances out to sea—blurts out.] A fine day we're having.

MILDRED—Is it?

SECOND ENGINEER—A nice warm breeze—

MILDRED—It feels cold to me.

SECOND ENGINEER—But it's hot enough in the sun—

MILDRED—Not hot enough for me. I don't like Nature. I was never athletic.

SECOND ENGINEER—[Forcing a smile.] Well, you'll find it hot enough where you're going.

MILDRED—Do you mean hell?

SECOND ENGINEER—[Flabbergasted, decides to laugh.] Ho-ho! No, I mean the stokehole.

MILDRED—My grandfather was a puddler. He played with boiling steel.

SECOND ENGINEER—[All at sea—uneasily.] Is that so? Hum, you'll excuse me, ma' am, but are you intending to wear that dress?

MILDRED—Why not?

SECOND ENGINEER—You'll likely rub against oil and dirt. It can't be helped.

MILDRED—It doesn't matter. I have lots of white dresses.

SECOND ENGINEER—I have an old coat you might throw over—

MILDRED—I have fifty dresses like this. I will throw this one into the sea when I come back. That ought to wash it clean, don't you think?

SECOND ENGINEER—[Doggedly.] There's ladders to climb down that are none too clean—and dark alleyways—

MILDRED—I will wear this very dress and none other.

SECOND ENGINEER—No offence meant. It's none of my business. I was only warning you—

MILDRED—Warning? That sounds thrilling.

SECOND ENGINEER—[Looking down the deck—with a sigh of relief.]—There's the Fourth now. He's waiting for us. If you'll come—

MILDRED—Go on. I'll follow you. [He goes. MILDRED

turns a mocking smile on her aunt.] An oaf—but a handsome, virile oaf.

AUNT—[Scornfully.] Poser!

MILDRED—Take care. He said there were dark alleyways—

AUNT—[In the same tone.] Poser!

MILDRED—[Biting her lips angrily.] You are right. But would that my millions were not so anemically chaste!

AUNT—Yes, for a fresh pose I have no doubt you would drag the name of Douglas in the gutter!

MILDRED—From which it sprang. Good-by, Aunt. Don't pray too hard that I may fall into the fiery furnace.

AUNT—Poser!

MILDRED—[Viciously.] Old hag! [She slaps her aunt insultingly across the face and walks off, laughing gaily.]

AUNT—[Screams after her.] I said poser!

[Curtain]

Scene III

The stokehole. A few minutes later

SCENE—The stokehole. In the rear, the dimly-outlined bulks of the furnaces and boilers. High overhead one hanging electric bulb sheds just enough light through the murky air laden with coal dust to pile up masses of shadows everywhere. A line of men, stripped to the waist, is before the furnace doors. They bend over, looking neither to right nor left, handling their shovels as if they were part of their bodies, with a strange, awkward, swinging rhythm. They use the shovels to throw open the furnace doors. Then from these fiery round holes in the black a flood of terrific light and heat pours full upon the men who are outlined in silhouette in the crouching, inhuman attitudes of chained gorillas. The men shovel with a rhythmic motion, swinging as on a pivot from the coal which lies in heaps on the floor behind to hurl it into the flaming mouths before them. There is a tumult of noise—the brazen clang of the furnace doors as they are flung open or slammed shut, the grating, teeth-gritting grind of steel against steel, of crunching coal. This clash of sounds stuns one's ears with its rending dissonance. But there is order in it, rhythm, a mechanical regulated recurrence, a tempo. And rising above all, making the air hum with the quiver of liberated energy, the roar of leaping flames in the furnaces, the monotonous throbbing beat of the engines.

As the curtain rises, the furnace doors are shut. The men are taking a breathing spell. One or two are arranging the coal behind them, pulling it into more accessible heaps. The others can be dimly made out leaning on their shovels in relaxed attitudes of exhaustion.

PADDY—[From somewhere in the line—plaintively.] Yerra, will this divil's own watch nivir end? Me back is broke. I'm destroyed entirely.

YANK—[From the center of the line—with exuberant scorn.] Aw, yuh make me sick! Lie down and croak, why don't yuh? Always beefin', dat's you! Say, dis is a cinch! Dis was made for me! It's my meat, get me! [A whistle is blown—a thin, shrill note from somewhere overhead in the darkness. YANK curses without resentment.] Dere's de damn engineer crakin' de whip. He tinks we're loafin'.

PADDY—[Vindictively.] God stiffen him!

YANK—[In an exultant tone of command.] Come on, youse guys! Git into de game! She's gittin' hungry! Pile some grub in her! Trow it into her belly! Come on now, all of youse! Open her up! [At this last all the men, who have followed his movements of getting into position, throw open their furnace doors with a deafening clang. The fiery light floods over their shoulders as they bend round for the coal. Rivulets of sooty sweat have traced maps on their backs. The enlarged muscles form bunches of high light and shadow.]

YANK—[Chanting a count as he shovels without seeming effort.] One-two-tree [His voice rising exultantly in the joy of battle.] Dat's de stuff! Let her have it! All togedder now! Sling it into her! Let her ride! Shoot de piece now! Call de toin on her! Drive her into it! Feel her move! Watch her smoke! Speed, dat's her middle name! Give her coal, youse guys! Coal, dat's her booze! Drink it up, baby! Let's see yuh sprint! Dig in and gain a lap! Dere she go-o-es [This last in the chanting formula of the gallery gods at the six-day bike race. He slams his furnace door shut. The others do likewise with as much unison as their wearied bodies will permit. The effect is of one fiery eye after another being blotted out with a series of accompanying bangs.]

PADDY—[Groaning.] Me back is broke. I'm bate out—bate—[There is a pause. Then the inexorable whistle sounds again from the dim regions above the electric light. There is a growl of cursing rage from all sides.]

YANK—[Shaking his fist upward—contemptuously.] Take it easy dere, you! Who d' yuh tinks runnin' dis game, me or you? When I git ready, we move. Not before! When I git ready, get me!

VOICES—[Approvingly.] That's the stuff!

Yank tal him, py golly!

Yank ain't affeerd.

Goot poy, Yank!

Give him hell!

Tell 'im' e's a bloody swine!

Bloody slave-driver!

YANK—[Contemptuously.] He ain't got no noive. He's yellow, get me? All de engineers is yellow. Dey got streaks a mile wide. Aw, to hell wit him! Let's move, youse guys. We had a rest. Come on, she needs it! Give her pep! It ain't for him. Him and his whistle, dey don't belong. But we belong, see! We gotter feed de baby! Come on! [He turns and flings his furnace door open. They all follow his lead. At this instant the SECOND and FOURTH ENGINEERS enter from the darkness on the left with MILDRED between them. She starts, turns paler, her pose is crumbling, she shivers with fright in spite of the blazing heat, but forces herself to leave the ENGINEERS and take a few steps nearer the men. She is right behind YANK. All this happens quickly while the men have their backs turned.]

YANK—Come on, youse guys! [He is turning to get coal when the whistle sounds again in a peremptory, irritating note. This drives YANK into a sudden fury. While the other men have turned full around and stopped dumfounded by the spectacle of MILDRED standing there in her white dress, YANK does not turn far enough to see her. Besides, his head is thrown back, he blinks upward through the murk trying to find the owner of the whistle, he brandishes his shovel murderously over his head in one hand, pounding on his chest, gorilla-like, with the other, shouting:] Toin off dat whistle! Come down outa dere, yuh yellow, brassbuttoned, Belfast bum, yuh! Come down and I'll knock yer brains out! Yuh lousey, stinkin', yellow mut of a Catholic-moiderin' bastard! Come down and I'll moider yuh! Pullin' dat whistle on me, huh? I'll show yuh! I'll crash yer skull in! I'll drive yer teet' down yer troat! I'll slam yer nose trou de back of yer head! I'll cut yer guts out for a nickel, yuh lousey boob, yuh dirty, crummy, muck-eatin' son of a— [Suddenly he becomes conscious of all the other men staring at something directly behind his back. He whirls defensively with a snarling, murderous growl, crouching to spring, his lips drawn back over his teeth, his small eyes gleaming ferociously. He sees MILDRED, like a white apparition in the full light from the open furnace doors. He glares into her eyes, turned to stone. As for her, during his speech she has listened, paralyzed with horror, terror, her whole personality crushed, beaten in, collapsed, by the terrific impact of this unknown, abysmal brutality, naked and shameless. As she looks at his gorilla face, as his eyes bore into hers, she utters a low, choking cry and shrinks away from him, putting both hands up before her eyes to shut out the sight of his face, to protect her own. This startles YANK to a reaction. His mouth falls open, his eyes grow bewildered.]

MILDRED—[About to faint—to the ENGINEERS, who now

have her one by each arm—whimperingly.] Take me away! Oh, the filthy beast! [She faints. They carry her quickly back, disappearing in the darkness at the left, rear. An iron door clangs shut. Rage and bewildered fury rush back on YANK. He feels himself insulted in some unknown fashion in the very heart of his pride. He roars:] God damn yuh! [And hurls his shovel after them at the door which has just closed. It hits the steel bulkhead with a clang and falls clattering on the steel floor. From overhead the whistle sounds again in a long, angry, insistent command.]

[Curtain]

Scene IV

Same as Scene I. Half an hour later.

SCENE—The firemen's forecastle. YANK's watch has just come off duty and had dinner. Their faces and bodies shine from a soap and water scrubbing but around their eyes, where a hasty dousing does not touch, the coal dust sticks like black make-up, giving them a queer, sinister expression. YANK has not washed either face or body. He stands out in contrast to them, a blackened, brooding figure. He is seated forward on a bench in the exact attitude of Rodin's "The Thinker." The others, most of them smoking pipes, are staring at YANK half-apprehensively, as if fearing an outburst; half-amusedly, as if they saw a joke somewhere that tickled them.

VOICES—He ain't ate nothin'.

Py golly, a fallar gat gat grub in him.

Divil a lie.

Yank feeda da fire, no feeda da face.

Ha-ha.

He ain't even washed hisself.

He's forgot.

Hey, Yank, you forgot to wash.

YANK—[Sullenly.] Forgot nothin'! To hell wit washin'.

VOICES—It'll stick to you.

It'll get under your skin.

Give yer the bleedin' itch, that's wot.

It makes spots on you—like a leopard.

Like a piebald nigger, you mean.

Better wash up, Yank.

You sleep better.

Wash up, Yank.

Wash up! Wash up!

YANK—[Resentfully.] Aw say, youse guys. Lemme alone. Can't youse see I'm tryin' to tink?

ALL—[Repeating the word after him as one with cynical mockery.] Think! [The word has a brazen, metallic quality as if their throats were phonograph horns. It is followed by a chorus of hard, barking laughter.]

YANK—[Springing to his feet and glaring at them belligerently.] Yes, tink! Tink, dat's what I said! What about it? [They are silent, puzzled by his sudden resentment at what used to be one of his jokes. YANK sits down again in the same attitude of "The Thinker."]

VOICES—Leave him alone. He's got a grouch on. Why wouldn't he?

PADDY—[With a wink at the others.] Sure I know what's the matther. 'Tis aisy to see. He's fallen in love, I'm telling you.

ALL—[Repeating the word after him as one with cynical mockery.] Love! [The word has a brazen, metallic quality as if their throats were phonograph horns. It is followed by a chorus of hard, barking laughter.]

YANK—[With a contemptuous snort.] Love, hell! Hate, dat's what. I've fallen in hate, get me?

PADDY—[Philosophically.] 'Twould take a wise man to tell one from the other. [With a bitter, ironical scorn, increasing as he goes on.] But I'm telling you it's love that's in it. Sure what else but love for us poor bastes in the stokehole would be bringing a fine lady, dressed like a white quane, down a mile of ladders and steps to be havin' a look at us? [A growl of anger goes up from all sides.]

LONG—[Jumping on a bench—hecticly.] Hinsultin' us! Hinsultin' us, the bloody cow! And them bloody engineers! What right 'as they got to be exhibitin' us 's if we was bleedin' monkeys in a menagerie? Did we sign for hinsults to our dignity as 'onest workers? Is that in the ship's articles? You kin bloody well bet it ain't! But I knows why they done it. I arsked a deck steward 'o she was and 'e told me. 'Er old man's a bleedin' millionaire, a bloody Capitalist! 'E's got enuf bloody gold to sink this bleedin' ship! 'E makes arf the bloody steel in the world! 'E owns this bloody boat! And you and me, comrades, we're 'is slaves! And the skipper and mates and engineers, they're 'is slaves! And she's 'is bloody daughter and we're all 'er slaves, too! And she gives 'er orders as' ow she wants to see the bloody animals below decks and down they takes' er! [There is a roar of rage from all sides.]

YANK—[Blinking at him bewilderedly.] Say! Wait a moment! Is all dat straight goods?

LONG—Straight as string! The bleedin' steward as waits on' em, ' e told me about 'er. And what're we goin' ter do, I arsks yer? ' Ave we got ter swaller' er hinsults like dogs? It ain't in the ship's articles. I tell yer we got a case. We kin go ter law—

YANK—[With abysmal contempt.] Hell! Law!

ALL—[Repeating the word after him as one with cynical mockery.] Law! [The word has a brazen metallic quality as if their throats were phonograph horns. It is followed by a chorus of hard, barking laughter.]

LONG—[Feeling the ground slipping from under his feet—desperately.] As voters and citizens we kin force the bloody governments—

YANK—[With abysmal contempt.] Hell! Governments!

ALL—[Repeating the word after him as one with cynical mockery.] Governments! [The word has a brazen metallic quality as if their throats were phonograph horns. It is followed by a chorus of hard, barking laughter.]

LONG—[Hysterically.] We're free and equal in the sight of God—

YANK—[With abysmal contempt.] Hell! God!

ALL—[Repeating the word after him as one with cynical mockery.] God! [The word has a brazen metallic quality as if their throats were phonograph horns. It is followed by a chorus of hard, barking laughter.]

YANK—[Witheringly.] Aw, join de Salvation Army!

ALL—Sit down! Shut up! Damn fool! Sea-lawyer! [Long slinks back out of sight.]

PADDY—[Continuing the trend of his thoughts as if he had never been interrupted—bitterly.] And there she was standing behind us, and the Second pointing at us like a man you'd hear in a circus would be saying: In this cage is a queerer kind of baboon than ever you'd find in darkest Africy. We roast them in their own sweat—and be damned if you won't hear some of thim saying they like it! [He glances scornfully at YANK.]

YANK—[With a bewildered uncertain growl.] Aw!

PADDY—And there was Yank roarin' curses and turning round wid his shovel to brain her—and she looked at him, and him at her—

YANK—[Slowly.] She was all white. I tought she was a ghost. Sure.

PADDY—[With heavy, biting sarcasm.] 'Twas love at first sight, divil a doubt of it! If you'd seen the endearin' look on her pale mug when she shrivelled away with her hands over her eyes to shut out the sight of him! Sure, 'twas as if she'd seen a great hairy ape escaped from the Zoo!

YANK—[Stung—with a growl of rage.] Aw!

PADDY—And the loving way Yank heaved his shovel at the skull of her, only she was out the door! [A grin breaking over his face.] 'Twas touching, I'm telling you! It put the touch of home, swate home in the stokehole. [There is a roar of laughter from all.]

YANK—[Glaring at PADDY menacingly.] Aw, choke dat off, see!

PADDY—[Not heeding him—to the others.] And her grabbin' at the Second's arm for protection. [With a grotesque imitation of a woman's voice.] Kiss me, Engineer dear, for it's dark down here and me old man's in Wall Street making money! Hug me tight, darlin', for I'm afeerd in the dark and me mother's on deck makin' eyes at the skipper! [Another roar of laughter.]

YANK—[Threateningly.] Say! What yuh tryin' to do, kid me, yuh old Harp?

PADDY—Divil a bit! Ain't I wishin' myself you'd brained her?

YANK—[Fiercely.] I'll brain her! I'll brain her yet, wait 'n' see! [Coming over to PADDY—slowly.] Say, is dat what she called me—a hairy ape?

PADDY—She looked it at you if she didn't say the word itself.

YANK—[Grinning horribly.] Hairy ape, huh? Sure! Dat's de way she looked at me, aw right. Hairy ape! So dat's me, huh? [Bursting into rage—as if she were still in front of him.] Yuh skinny tart! Yuh white-faced bum, yuh! I'll show yuh who's a ape! [Turning to the others, bewilderment seizing him again.] Say, youse guys. I was bawlin' him out for pullin' de whistle on us. You heard me. And den I seen youse lookin' at somep'n and I tought he'd sneaked down to come up in back of me, and I hopped round to knock him dead wit de shovel. And dere she was wit de light on her! Christ, yuh coulda pushed me over with a finger! I was scared, get me? Sure! I tought she was a ghost, see? She was all in white like dey wrap around stiffs. You seen her. Kin yuh blame me? She didn't belong, dat's what. And den when I come to and seen it was a real skoit and seen de way she was lookin' at me—like Paddy said—Christ, I was sore, get me? I don't stand for dat stuff from nobody. And I flung de shovel—on'y she'd beat it. [Furiously.] I wished it'd banged her! I wished it'd knocked her block off!

LONG—And be 'anged for murder or 'lectrocuted? She ain't bleedin' well worth it.

YANK—I don't give a damn what! I'd be square wit her, wouldn't I? Tink I wanter let her put somep'n over on me? Tink I'm goin' to let her git away wit dat stuff? Yuh don't know me! Noone ain't never put nothin' over on me and got away wit it, see! —not dat kind of stuff—no guy and no skoit neither! I'll fix her! Maybe she'll come down again—

VOICE—No chance, Yank. You scared her out of a year's growth.

YANK—I scared her? Why de hell should I scare her? Who de hell is she? Ain't she de same as me? Hairy ape, huh? [With his old confident bravado.] I'll show her I'm better'n her, if she on'y knew it. I belong and she don't, see! I move and she's dead! Twenty-five knots a hour, dats me! Dat carries her but I make dat. She's on'y baggage. Sure! [Again bewilderedly.] But, Christ, she was funny lookin'! Did yuh pipe her hands? White and skinny. Yuh could see de bones trough 'em. And her mush, dat was dead white, too. And her eyes, dey was like dey'd seen a ghost. Me, dat was! Sure! Hairy ape! Ghost, huh? Look at dat arm! [He extends his right arm, swelling out the great muscles.] I coulda took her wit dat, wit' just my little finger even, and broke her in two. [Again bewilderedly.] Say, who is dat skoit, huh? What is she? What's she come from? Who made her? Who give her de noive to look at me like dat? Dis ting's got my goat right. I don't get her. She's new to me. What does a skoit like her mean, huh? She don't belong, get me! I can't see her. [With growing anger.] But one ting I'm wise to, aw right, aw right! Youse all kin bet your shoits I'll git even wit her. I'll show her if she tinks she—She grinds de organ and I'm on de string, huh? I'll fix her! Let her come down again and I'll fling her in de furnace! She'll move den! She won't shiver at nothin', den! Speed, dat'll be her! She'll belong den! [He grins horribly.]

PADDY—She'll never come. She's had her belly-full, I'm telling you. She'll be in bed now, I'm thinking, wid ten doctors and nurses feedin' her salts to clean the fear out of her.

YANK—[Enraged.] Yuh tink I made her sick, too, do yuh? Just lookin' at me, huh? Hairy ape, huh? [In a frenzy of rage.] I'll fix her! I'll tell her where to git off! She'll git down on her knees and take it back or I'll bust de face offen her! [Shaking one fist upward and beating on his chest with the other.] I'll find yuh! I'm comin', d'yuh hear? I'll fix yuh, God damn yuh! [He makes a rush for the door.]

VOICES—Stop him!

He'll get shot!

He'll murder her!

Trip him up!

Hold him!

He's gone crazy!

Gott, he's strong!

Hold him down!

Look out for a kick!

Pin his arms!

[They have all piled on him and, after a fierce struggle, by sheer weight of numbers have borne him to the floor just inside the door.]

PADDY—[Who has remained detached.] Kape him down till he's cooled off. [Scornfully.] Yerra, Yank, you're a great fool. Is it payin' attention at all you are to the like of that skinny sow widout one drop of rale blood in her?

YANK—[Frenziedly, from the bottom of the heap.] She done me doit! She done me doit, didn't she? I'll git square with her! I'll get her some way! Git offen me, youse guys! Lemme up! I'll show her who's a ape!

[Curtain]

IV

Emily Bronte

4.1 The Introductory Remarks of Emily Bronte

Emily Bronte is an excellent woman novelist and poet in the Victorian age. She shares the same fame on novel writing with her sister Charlotte Bronte. Her novel *Wuthering Heights* brings her great reputation.

In her childhood, listening to the ancient Irish legends told by her father, roaming the out-of-the-way moor in Yorkshire, Emily's imagination and artistic competence were nurtured. She had a great hatred of the authority of the school that maltreated the poor children there and left school in rage. Thereafter, she and Charlotte went to Brussels for further study. After the death of their aunt, she stayed home as the housekeeper. Then she tried writing poems and other works. In 1847, Emily's *Wuthering Heights* was completed. It appealed to the interests of readers because of its interwoven theme of love and revenge, its well-known plot and passionate and powerful language. Unluckily, when Emily attempted to celebrate the publication of this book, serious disease took her life.

4.2 Comment on *Wuthering Heights*

Wuthering Heights is generally believed as one of the most remarkable novels written by the Bronte sisters. Emily uses her delicate pen to depict an odd love story and portray Heathcliff, the hero's turbulent passion and hatred. Through Heathcliff's experience, the authoress makes her severe attitude towards the social inequality caused by the class hierarchies and prejudice.

The narration of the novel is designed in a unique way. It is told to narrator, Mr. Lockwood, the lodger of Thrushcross Grange by Ellen "Nelly" Dean, the housekeeper of both Wuthering Heights and Thrushcross Grange, with frequent use of flashback. At the beginning of the story, Mr. Lockwood comes to Wuthering Heights for his rent. Owning to the heavy snow, he stays for night there. After having a ghost-haunted experience, he makes his inquiry of Ellen "Nelly" Dean, the second narrator who gives her account of the story between Heathcliff, the hero, and Catherine, the heroine.

Many years ago, the original owner of Wuthering Heights, Mr. Earnshaw picks up Heathcliff, a boy from Liverpool and treats him as his own child. Heathcliff becomes Mr. Earnshaw's daughter, Catherine's bosom friend. But his coming annoys Mr. Earnshaw's son Hindley. After the death of Mr. Earnshaw, Hindley begins to torture Heathcliff. One day, Catherine encounters the elegant Edgar

Linton, the young owner of Thrushcross Grange for she wounds herself near Thrushcross Grange. Afterwards she accepts Linton's marriage proposal. Being irritated and despaired, Heathcliff leaves Wuthering Heights.

Three years later, Heathcliff comes back secretly and begins his revenge. He lends heavy loan to Hindley and induces Edgar's sister Isabella, whom he abuses. Catherine gets very ill, for Heathcliff's passion has worsen her condition. So after giving birth to her daughter Cathy, she dies. Twelve years passes. Healthcliff successfully gains the control of both Wuthering Heights from Hindley and Thrushcross Grange from Linton. He enslaves and maltreats Hareton, Hindley's son in revenge for his humiliation given by Hindley and forces Cathy to marry his seriously ill son, who dies soon.

Facing the intimate relationship between Hareton and Cathy, the humanity in Heathcliff awakens. He abandons his revenge and begins to dream of reuniting with Catherine in the graveyard.

This selection is taken from the last chapter of the novel. It mainly tells that Heathcliff becomes aware of the love between Cathy and Hareton. His humanity has been called back. He stops his act of taking revenge. Since then, his only wish is to meet Catherine and earnestly wait for the coming of his death. Finally his dream comes true. He has been found dead in his bed on a windy and rainy night. After his death, he is buried next to Catherine in the graveyard(Edgar's grave is on the other side of Catherine's), and there is a rumor in the village that their ghosts can be seen wandering together on the moors.

4.3 The Text of *Wuthering Heights*

Chapter 34

For some days after that evening, Mr. Heathcliff shunned meeting us at meals; yet he would not consent formally to exclude Hareton and Cathy. He had an aversion to yielding so completely to his feelings, choosing rather to absent himself; and eating once in twenty-four hours seemed sufficient sustenance for him.

One night, after the family were in bed, I heard him go downstairs, and out at the front door. I did not hear him re-enter, and in the morning I found he was still away. We were in April then: the weather was sweet and warm, the grass as green as showers and sun could make it, and the two dwarf apple trees near the southern wall in full bloom. After breakfast, Catherine insisted on my bringing a chair and sitting with my work under the fir trees at the end of the house; and she beguiled Hareton, who had perfectly recovered from his accident, to dig and arrange her little garden, which was shifted to that corner by the influence of Joseph's complaints. I was comfortably revelling in the spring fragrance around, and the beautiful soft blue overhead, when my young lady, who had run down near the gate to procure some primrose roots for a border, returned only half laden, and informed us that Mr. Heathcliff was coming in. "And he spoke to me," she added, with a perplexed countenance.

"What did he say?" asked Hareton.

"He told me to begone as fast as I could," she answered. "But he looked so different from his usual look that I stopped a moment to stare at him."

"How?" he inquired.

"Why, almost bright and cheerful. No, almost nothing—very much excited, and wild and glad!" she replied.

"Night walking amuses him, then," I remarked, affecting a careless manner: in reality as surprised as she was, and anxious to ascertain the truth of her statement; for to see the master looking glad would not be an everyday spectacle. I framed an excuse to go in. Heathcliff stood at the open door, he was pale, and he trembled: yet, certainly, he had a strange, joyful glitter in his eyes, that altered the aspect of his whole face.

"Will you have some breakfast?" I said. "You must be hungry, rambling about all night!" I wanted to discover where he had been, but I did not like to ask directly.

"No, I'm not hungry," he answered, averting his head, and speaking rather contemptuously, as if he guessed I was trying to divine the occasion of his good humour.

I felt perplexed: I didn't know whether it were not a proper opportunity to offer a bit of admonition.

"I don't think it right to wander out of doors," I observed, "instead of being in bed: it is not wise, at any rate, this moist season. I dare say you'll catch a bad cold, or a fever: you have something the matter with you now!"

"Nothing but what I can bear," he replied; "and with the greatest pleasure, provided you'll leave me alone; get in, and don't annoy me."

I obeyed: and, in passing, I noticed he breathed as fast as a cat.

"Yes!" I reflected to myself, "we shall have a fit of illness. I cannot conceive what he has been doing."

That noon he sat down to dinner with us, and received a heaped-up plate from my hands, as if he intended to make amends for previous fasting.

"I've neither cold nor fever, Nelly," he remarked, in allusion to my morning's speech; "and I'm ready to do justice to the food you give me."

He took his knife and fork, and was going to commence eating, when the inclination appeared to become suddenly extinct. He laid them on the table, looked eagerly towards the window, then rose and went out. "We saw him walking to and fro in the garden while we concluded our meal, and Earnshaw said he'd go and ask why he would not dine: he thought we had grieved him some way."

"Well, is he coming?" cried Catherine, when her cousin returned.

"Nay," he answered; "but he's not angry: he seemed rare and pleased indeed; only I made him impatient by speaking to him twice; and then he bid me be off to you: he wondered how I could want the company of anybody else."

I set his plate to keep warm on the fender; and after an hour or two he re-entered, when the room was clear, in no degree calmer: the same unnatural—it was unnatural—appearance of joy under his black brows; the same bloodless hue, and his teeth visible, now and then, in a kind of smile; his frame shivering, not as one shivers with chill or weakness, but as a tight-stretched cord vibrates—a strong thrilling, rather than trembling.

I will ask what is the matter, I thought; or who should? And I exclaimed:

"Have you heard any good news, Mr. Heathcliff? You look uncommonly animated."

"Where should good news come from to me?" he said. "I'm animated with hunger; and, seemingly, I must not eat."

"Your dinner is here," I returned; "why won't you get it?"

"I don't want it now;" he muttered hastily; "I'll wait till supper. And, Nelly, once for all, let me beg you to warn Hareton and the other away from me. I wish to be troubled by nobody; I wish to have this place to myself."

"Is there some new reason for this banishment?" I inquired. "Tell me why you are so queer, Mr. Heathcliff? Where were you last night? I'm not putting the question through idle curiosity, but—"

"You are putting the question through very idle curiosity," he interrupted, with a laugh. "Yet I'll answer it. Last night I was on the threshold of hell. Today, I am within sight of my heaven. I have my eyes on it: hardly three feet to sever me! And now you'd better go! You'll neither see nor hear anything to frighten you, if you refrain from prying."

Having swept the hearth and wiped the table, I departed; more perplexed than ever.

He did not quit the house again that afternoon, and no one intruded on his solitude; till, at eight o'clock, I deemed it proper, though unsummoned, to carry a candle and his supper to him. He was leaning against the ledge of an open lattice, but not looking out: his face was turned to the interior gloom. The fire had smouldered to ashes; the room was filled with the damp, mild air of the cloudy evening; and so still, that not only the murmur of the beck down Gimmerton was distinguishable, but its ripples and its gurgling over the pebbles, or through the large stones which it could not cover. I uttered an ejaculation of discontent at seeing the dismal grate, and commenced shutting the casements, one after another, till I came to his.

"Must I close this?" I asked, in order to rouse him; for he would not stir.

The light flashed on his features as I spoke. Oh, Mr. Lockwood, I cannot express what a terrible start I got by the momentary view! Those deep black eyes! That smile, and ghastly paleness! It appeared to me, not Mr. Heathcliff, but a goblin; and, in my terror, I let the candle bend towards the wall, and it left me in darkness.

"Yes, close it," he replied, in his familiar voice. "There, that is pure awkwardness! Why did you hold the candle horizontally? Be quick, and bring another."

I hurried out in a foolish state of dread, and said to Joseph: "The master wishes you to take him a light and rekindle the fire."

For I dare not go in myself again just then.

Joseph rattled some fire into the shovel, and went; but he brought it back immediately, with the supper tray in his other hand, explaining that Mr. Heathcliff was going to bed, and he wanted nothing to eat till morning. We heard him mount the stairs directly; he did not proceed to his ordinary chamber, but turned into that with the panelled bed: its window, as I mentioned before, is wide enough for anybody to get through; and it struck me that he plotted another midnight excursion, of which he had rather we had no suspicion.

"Is he a ghoul or a vampire?" I mused. I had read of such hideous incarnate demons. And then I set myself to reflect how I had tended him in infancy, and watched him grow to youth, and followed him almost through his whole course; and what absurd nonsense it was to yield to that sense of horror. "But where did he come from, the little dark thing, harboured by a good man to his bane?" muttered Superstition, as I dozed into unconsciousness. And I began, half dreaming, to weary myself with imagining some fit parentage for him; and, repeating my waking meditations, I tracked his existence over again, with grim variations; at last, picturing his death and funeral: of which, all I can remember is, being exceedingly vexed at having the task of dictating an inscription for his monument, and consulting the sexton about it; and, as he had no surname, and we could not tell his age, we were obliged to content ourselves with the single word, "Heathcliff". That came true: we were. If you enter the kirkyard, you'll read on his headstone, only that, and the date of his death.

Dawn restored me to common sense. I rose, and went into the garden, as soon as I could see, to ascertain if there were any footmarks under his window. There were none. "He has stayed at home—ought, and he'll be all right today. "I prepared breakfast for the household, as was my usual custom, but told Hareton and Catherine to get theirs ere the master came down, for he lay late. They preferred taking it out of doors, under the trees, and I set a little table to accommodate them.

On my re-entrance, I found Mr. Heathcliff below. He and Joseph were conversing about some farming business; he gave clear, minute directions concerning the matter discussed, but he spoke rapidly, and turned his head continually aside, and had the same excited expression, even more exaggerated. When Joseph quitted the room he took his seat in the place he generally chose, and I put a basin of coffee before him. He drew it nearer, and then rested his arms on the table, and looked at the opposite wall, as I supposed, surveying one particular portion, up and down, with glittering, restless eyes, and with such eager interest that he stopped breathing during half a minute together.

"Come now," I exclaimed, pushing some bread against his hand, "eat and drink that, while it is hot: it has been waiting near an hour."

He didn't notice me, and yet he smiled. I'd rather have seen him gnash his teeth than smile so.

"Mr. Heathcliff! master!" I cried, "don't, for God's sake, stare as if you saw an unearthly vision."

"Don't, for God's sake, shout so loud," he replied. "Turn round, and tell me, are we by ourselves?"

"Of course," was my answer; "of course we are."

Still I involuntarily obeyed him, as if I were not quite sure. "With a sweep of his hand he cleared a vacant space in front among the breakfast things, and leant forward to gaze more at his ease.

Now, I perceived he was not looking at the wall; for when I regarded him alone, it seemed exactly that he gazed at something within two yards' distance. And whatever it was, it communicated, apparently, both pleasure and pain in exquisite extremes: at least the anguished, yet raptured, expression of his countenance suggested that idea. The fancied object was not fixed: either his eyes pursued it with unwearied diligence, and, even in speaking to me, were never weaned away. I vainly reminded him of his protracted abstinence from food: if he stirred to touch anything in compliance with my entreaties, if he stretched his hand out to get a piece of bread, his fingers clenched before they reached it, and remained on the table, forgetful of their aim.

I sat, a model of patience, trying to attract his absorbed attention from its engrossing speculation; till he grew irritable, and got—up, asking why I would not allow him to have his own time in taking his meals? And saying that on the next occasion, I needn't wait: I might set the things down and go. Having uttered these words he left the house, slowly sauntered down the garden path, and disappeared through the gate.

The hours crept anxiously by: another evening came. I did not retire to rest till late, and when I did, I could not sleep. He returned after midnight, and, instead of going to bed, shut himself into the room beneath. I listened, and tossed about, and, finally, dressed and descended. It was too irksome to lie up there, harassing my brain with a hundred idle misgivings.

I distinguished Mr. Heathcliff's step, restlessly measuring the floor, and he frequently broke the silence by a deep inspiration, resembling a groan. He muttered detached words also; the only one I could catch was the name of Catherine, coupled with some wild term of endearment or suffering; and spoken as one would speak to a person present: low and earnest, and wrung from the depth of his soul. I had not courage to walk straight into the apartment; but I desired to divert him from his reverie, and therefore fell foul of the kitchen fire, stirred it, and began to scrape the cinders. It drew him forth sooner than I expected. He opened the door immediately, and said:

"Nelly, come here—is it morning? Come in with your light."

"It is striking four," I answered. "You want a candle to take upstairs: you might have lit one at this fire."

"No, I don't wish to go upstairs," he said. "Come in, and kindle me a fire, and do anything there is to do about the room."

"I must blow the coals red first, before I can carry any," I replied, getting a chair and the bellows.

He roamed to and fro, meantime, in a state approaching distraction; his heavy sighs succeeding each other so thick as to leave no space for common breathing between.

"When day breaks I'll send for Green," he said; "I wish to make some legal inquiries of him while I can bestow a thought on those matters, and while I can act calmly. I have not written my will yet; and how to leave my property I cannot determine. I wish I could annihilate it from the face of the earth."

"I would not talk so, Mr. Heathcliff," I interposed. "Let your will be a while: you'll be spared to repent of your many injustices yet. I never expected that your nerves would be disordered: they are, at present, marvellously so, however; and almost entirely through your own fault. The way you've passed these three last days might knock up a Titan. Do take some food, and some repose. You need only look at yourself in a glass to see how you require both. Your cheeks are hollow, and your eyes bloodshot, like a person starving with hunger and going blind with loss of sleep."

"It is not my fault that I cannot eat or rest," he replied. "I assure you it is through no settled designs. I'll do both as soon as I possibly can. But you might as well bid a man struggling in the water rest within arm's length of the shore! I must reach it first, and then I'll rest. Well, never mind Mr. Green: as to repenting of my injustices, I've done no injustice, and I repent of nothing. I'm too happy; and yet I'm not happy enough. My soul's bliss kills my body, but does not satisfy itself."

"Happy, master?" I cried. "Strange happiness! If you would hear me without being angry, I might offer some advice that would make you happier."

"What is that?" he asked. "Give it."

"You are aware, Mr. Heathcliff," I said, "that from the time you were thirteen years old, you have lived a selfish, unchristian life; and probably hardly had a Bible in your hands during all that period. You must have forgotten the contents of the book, and you may not have space to search it now. Could it be hurtful to send for someone—some minister of any denomination, it does not matter which—to explain it, and show you how very far you have erred from its precepts; and how unfit you will be for its heaven, unless a change takes place before you die?"

"I'm rather obliged than angry, Nelly," he said, "for you remind me of the manner that I desire to be buried in. It is to be carried to the churchyard in the evening. You and Hareton may, if you please, accompany me: and mind, particularly, to notice that the sexton obeys my directions concerning the two coffins! No minister need come; nor need anything be said over me. —I tell you I have nearly attained my heaven; and that of others is altogether unvalued and uncovered by me."

"And supposing you persevered in your obstinate fast, and died by that means, and they refused to bury you in the precincts of the kirk?" I said, shocked at his godless indifference. "How would you like it?"

"They won't do that," he replied, "if they did, you must have me removed secretly: and if you neglect it you shall prove, practically, that the dead are not annihilated!"

As soon as he heard the other members of the family stirring he retired to his den, and I breathed freer. But in the afternoon, while Joseph and Hareton were at their work, he came into the kitchen again, and, with a wild look, bid me come and sit in the house: he wanted somebody with him. I declined: telling him plainly that his strange talk and manner frightened me, and I had neither the nerve nor the will to be his companion alone.

"I believe you think me a fiend," he said, with his dismal laugh: something too horrible to live under a decent roof. Then turning to Catherine, who was there, and who drew behind me at his approach, he added, half sneeringly—"Will you come, chuck? I'll not hurt you. No! to you I've made myself worse than the devil. Well, there is one who won't shrink from my company! By God! she's relentless. Oh, damn it! It's unutterably too much for flesh and blood to bear—even mine."

He solicited the society of no one more. At dusk, he went into his chamber. Through the whole night, and far into the morning, we heard him groaning and murmuring to himself. Hareton was anxious to enter; but I bade him fetch Mr. Kenneth, and he should go in and see him. When he came, and I requested admittance and tried to open the door, I found it locked; and Heathcliff bid us be damned. He was better, and would be left alone; so the doctor went away.

The following evening was very wet: indeed it poured down till day-dawn; and, as I took my morning walk round the house, I observed the master's window swinging open, and the rain driving straight in. He cannot be in bed, I thought: those showers would drench him through. He must either be up or out. But I'll make no more ado, I'll go boldly and look.

Having succeeded in obtaining entrance with another key, I ran to unclose the panels, for the chamber was vacant; quickly pushing them aside, I peeped in. Mr. Heathcliff was there—laid on his back. His eyes met mine so keen and fierce, I started; and then he seemed to smile. I could not think him dead: but his face and throat were washed with rain; the bedclothes dripped, and he was perfectly still. The lattice, flapping to and fro, had grazed one hand that rested on the sill; no blood trickled from the broken skin, and when I put my fingers to it, I could doubt no more: he was dead and stark!

I hasped the window; I combed his black long hair from his forehead; I tried to close his eyes: to extinguish, if possible, that frightful, lifelike gaze of exultation before anyone else beheld it. They would not shut: they seemed to sneer at my attempts: and his parted lips and sharp white teeth sneered too! Taken with another fit of cowardice, I cried out for Joseph. Joseph shuffled up and made a noise; but resolutely refused to meddle with him.

"Th' divil's harried off his soul," he cried, "and he muh hev his carcass intuh t'bargain, for ow't Aw care! Ech! What a wicked un he looks girning at death!" And the old sinner grinned in mockery. I thought he intended to cut a caper round the bed; but, suddenly composing himself, he fell on his knees, and raised his hands, and returned thanks that the lawful master and the ancient stock were restored to their rights.

I felt stunned by the awful event; and my memory unavoidably recurred to former times with a sort of oppressive sadness. But poor Hareton, the most wronged, was the only one that really suffered much. He sat by the corpse all night, weeping in bitter earnest. He pressed its hand, and kissed the sarcastic savage face that everyone else shrank from contemplating; and bemoaned him with that strong grief which springs naturally from a generous heart, though it be tough as tempered steel.

Mr. Kenneth was perplexed to pronounce of what disorder the master died. I concealed the fact of his having swallowed nothing for four days, fearing it might lead to trouble, and then, I am persuaded, he did not abstain on purpose: it was the consequence of his strange illness, not the cause.

We buried him, to the scandal of the whole neighbourhood, as he wished. Earnshaw and I, the sexton, and six men to carry the coffin, comprehended the whole attendance. The six men departed when they had let it down into the grave: we stayed to see it covered. Hareton, with a streaming face, dug green sods, and laid them over the brown mould himself: at present it is as smooth and verdant as its companion mounds—and I hope its tenant sleeps as soundly. But the country folk, if you ask them, would swear on the Bible that he walks: there are those who speak to having met him near the church, and on the moor, and even in this house. Idle tales, you'll say, and so say I. Yet that old man by the kitchen fire affirms he has seen two on 'em, looking out of his chamber window, on every rainy night since his death: and an odd thing happened to me about a month ago. I was going to the Grange one evening—a dark evening, threatening thunder—and, just at the turn of the Heights, I encountered a little boy with a sheep and two lambs before him; he was crying terribly; and I supposed the lambs were skittish, and would not be guided.

"What's the matter, my little man?" I asked.

"There's Heathcliff and a woman, yonder, under t'nab," he blubbered, "un' I darnut pass 'em."

I saw nothing; but neither the sheep nor he would go on; so I bid him take the road lower down. He probably raised the phantoms from thinking, as he traversed the moors alone, on the nonsense he had heard his parents and companions repeat. Yet, still, I don't like being out in the dark now; and I don't like being left by myself in this grim house: I cannot help it; I shall be glad when they leave it, and shift to the Grange.

"They are going to the Grange, then," I said.

"Yes," answered Mrs. Dean, "is soon as they are married, and that will be on New Year's Day."

"And who will live here, then?"

"Why, Joseph will take care of the house, and, perhaps, a lad to keep him company. They will live in the kitchen, and the rest will be shut up."

"For the use of such ghosts as choose to inhabit it," I observed.

"No, Mr. Lockwood," said Nelly, shaking her head. "I believe the dead are at peace: but it is not right to speak of them with levity."

At that moment the garden gate swung to; the ramblers were returning.

"They are afraid of nothing," I grumbled, watching their approach through the window. "Together they would brave Satan and all his legions."

As they stepped on to the doorstones, and halted to take a last look at the moon—or, more correctly, at each other by her light—I felt irresistibly impelled to escape them again; and, pressing a remembrance into the hand of Mrs. Dean, and disregarding her expostulations at my rudeness, I vanished through the kitchen as they opened the house-door; and so should have confirmed Joseph in his opinion of his fellow-servant's gay indiscretions, had he not fortunately recognized me for a respectable character by the sweet ring of a sovereign at his feet.

My walk home was lengthened by a diversion in the direction of the kirk. When beneath its walls, I perceived decay had made progress, even in seven months: many a window showed black gaps deprived of glass; and slates jutted off, here and there, beyond the right line of the roof, to be gradually worked off in coming autumn storms.

I sought, and soon discovered, the three headstones on the slope next the moor: the middle one grey, and half buried in heath: Edgar Linton's only harmonized by the turf and moss creeping up its foot: Heathcliff's still bare.

I lingered round them, under that benign sky; watched the moths fluttering among the heath and harebells, listened to the soft wind breathing through the grass, and wondered how anyone could ever imagine unquiet slumbers for the sleepers in that quiet earth.

Oscar Wilde

5.1 The Introductory Remarks of Oscar Wilde

Oscar Wilde is one of the important representatives of English Aesthetic Movement in the 19th century. He is a versatile writer. In addition to plays and essays, he creates a variety of poems, and fairy stories. His works reflect the cultural crisis of English society in his time. Wilde's plays are featured with well designed plots, humorous characters and refined language, which establish his high position in English plays in the 19th century. As a leader of the English Aestheticism Wilde acts as his fundamental theory of "art for art's sake." He believes that art is above life and that art should not be judged by moral, political or other non-aesthetic standards. His view of art criticism has been thoroughly embodied in his literary works.

Oscar Wilde was born in Dublin in a doctor's family in 1836.

When he grew up, he went to England, attending Oxford for study. Influenced by the aesthetic movement flourishing in Europe, Wilde was absorbed in English essayists Ruskin and Pater's aesthetic doctrine and put it into use, then developed his own aesthetic viewpoint. Wilde's artist point of view can be perceived in his only novel *The Picture of Dorian Gray* and his celebrated essay *The Decay of Lying*(1889).

Wilde is a prolific writer. In all his life he has authored many famous comedies on the topic of social issues such as *Lady Windermere's Fan*(1893), *A Woman of No Importance*(1894), *An Ideal Husband* and *The Importance of Being Earnest*(1895). In these plays Wilde exposes the emptiness of the nobleman's social life as well as their flirting, wretched appearance, making his sharpening criticism of dukes and ladies from the corrupted high society. *Salome* is Wilde's well-known tragedy which represents his highest achievement. In 1881 Wilde published a collection of fairy stories titled *The House of Pomegranates.* Ten years later he completed his two collection of fairy stories *The Happy Prince* and *Other Tales*. His fairy stories reveal his sympathy for poor and his pursuit for the true, the good, and the beautiful. The novel *The Picture of Dorian Gray* is Wilde's another important work, and he makes account of a process of how Dorian, an innocent young man degenerates into a hedonist. In the novel the author presents his theory: art is above life.

5.2 Comment on *The Picture of Dorian Gray*

The Picture of Dorian Gray is Oscar Wilde's only novel. In this novel the author intends to unfold his aesthetic point of view to readers by depicting the process of how Dorian, the protagonist who is a handsome and innocent young man, degenerates himself into an evil hedonist.

At the beginning of the novel, by chance Dorian invites a painter Howard to draw a portrait for him. From this picture he comes to realize his handsomeness and takes pride in it. Induced by Lord Herry Watton's pleasure-seeking doctrine, Dorian indulges himself in his own delights and in depravities, committing many crimes. His notorious behaviors are marked on his portrait slightly. To seek for his pleasure he deserts his lover, leading to her committing suicide. Out of his selfishness and envy, he murders his bosom friend. At the same time he tempts many naive young people to follow him, leading to their degeneration. His crimes are left the ferocious marks on the face of his portrait, Dorian could not resist in such ugly marks, thus he stabs his picture becoming a corpse, while his picture restores its original handsomeness and innocence. Wilde tries to present his different aesthetic point of view through his portrayal of his protagonist's life experience.

In *The Picture of Dorian Gray*, Wilde first shows off the three levels of artist beauty and the protagonists' seek for such beauty. Dorian attempts to gain his pure physical beauty at the mercy of taking others' love and life. Howard searches for his sexual beauty by the means of pleasure-seeking. Their seek for beauty is above reality they should face. Apparently the author adheres to such viewpoint that an aesthete should take his responsibility for making a study of his sensibility based on his diverse sensuous and passionate experience to create his artist work. Wilde seems to condemn the evils of self-regarding hedonism with his elegant style of writing in *The Picture of Dorian Gray*.

5.3 The Text of *The Picture of Dorian Gray*

Chapter 1

The studio was filled with the rich odour of roses, and when the light summer wind stirred amidst the trees of the garden, there came through the open door the heavy scent of the lilac, or the more delicate perfume of the pink-flowering thorn.

From the corner of the divan of Persian saddle-bags on which he was lying, smoking, as was his custom, innumerable cigarettes, Lord Henry Wotton could just catch the gleam of the honey-sweet and honey-coloured blossoms of a laburnum, whose tremulous branches seemed hardly able to bear the burden of a beauty so flamelike as theirs; and now and then the fantastic shadows of birds in flight flitted across the long tussore-silk curtains that were stretched in front of the huge window, producing a kind of momentary Japanese effect, and making him think of those pallid, jade-faced painters of Tokyo who, through the medium of an art that is necessarily immobile, seek to convey the sense of swiftness and motion. The sullen murmur of the bees shouldering their way through the long unmown grass, or circling with monotonous insistence round the dusty gilt horns of the straggling woodbine, seemed to make the stillness more oppressive. The dim roar of London was like the bourdon note of a distant organ.

In the centre of the room, clamped to an upright easel, stood the full-length portrait of a young man of extraordinary personal beauty, and in front of it, some little distance away, was sitting the artist himself, Basil Hallward, whose sudden disappearance some years ago caused, at the time, such public excitement and gave rise to so many strange conjectures.

As the painter looked at the gracious and comely form he had so skilfully mirrored in his art, a smile of pleasure passed across his face, and seemed about to linger there. But he suddenly started up, and closing his eyes, placed his fingers upon the lids, as though he sought to imprison within his brain some curious dream from which he feared he might awake.

"It is your best work, Basil, the best thing you have ever done," said Lord Henry languidly. "You must certainly send it next year to the Grosvenor. The Academy is too large and too vulgar. Whenever I have gone there, there have been either so many people that I have not been able to see the pictures, which was dreadful, or so many pictures that I have not been able to see the people, which was worse. The Grosvenor is really the only place."

"I don't think I shall send it anywhere," he answered, tossing his head back in that odd way that used to make his friends laugh at him at Oxford. "No, I won't send it anywhere."

Lord Henry elevated his eyebrows and looked at him in amazement through the thin blue wreaths of smoke that curled up in such fanciful whorls from his heavy, opium-tainted cigarette. "Not send it anywhere? My dear fellow, why? Have you any reason? What odd chaps you painters are! You do anything in the world to gain a reputation. As soon as you have one, you seem to want to throw it away. It is silly of you, for there is only one thing in the world worse than being talked about, and that is not being talked about. A portrait like this would set you far above all the young men in England, and make the old men quite jealous, if old men are ever capable of any emotion."

"I know you will laugh at me," he replied, "but I really can't exhibit it. I have put too much of myself into it."

Lord Henry stretched himself out on the divan and laughed. "Yes, I knew you would; but it is quite true, all the same." "Too much of yourself in it! Upon my word, Basil, I didn't know you were so vain; and I really can't see any resemblance between you, with your rugged strong face and your coal-black hair, and this young Adonis, who looks as if he was made out of ivory and rose-leaves. Why, my dear Basil, he is a Narcissus, and you—well, of course you have an intellectual expression and all that. But beauty, real beauty, ends where an intellectual expression begins. Intellect is in itself a mode of exaggeration, and destroys the harmony of any face. The moment one sits down to think, one becomes all nose, or all forehead, or something horrid. Look at the successful men in any of the learned professions. How perfectly hideous they are! Except, of course, in the Church. But then in the Church they don't think. A bishop keeps on saying at the age of eighty what he was told to say when he was a boy of eighteen, and as a natural consequence he always looks absolutely delightful. Your mysterious young friend, whose name you have never told me, but whose picture really fascinates me, never thinks. I feel quite sure of that. He is some brainless beautiful creature who should be always here in winter when we have no flowers to look at, and always here in summer when we want something to chill our intelligence. Don't flatter yourself, Basil: you are not in the least like him."

"You don't understand me, Harry," answered the artist. "Of course I am not like him. I know that perfectly well. Indeed, I should be sorry to look like him. You shrug your shoulders? I am telling you the truth. There is a fatality about all physical and intellectual distinction, the sort of fatality that seems to dog through history the faltering steps of kings. It is better not to be different from one's fellows. The ugly and the stupid have the best of it in this world. They can sit at their ease and gape at the play. If they know nothing of victory, they are at least spared the knowledge of defeat. They live as we all should live—undisturbed, indifferent, and without disquiet. They neither bring ruin upon others, nor ever receive it from alien hands. Your rank and wealth, Harry; my brains, such as they are—my art, whatever it may be worth; Dorian Gray's good looks—we shall all suffer for what the gods have given us, suffer terribly."

"Dorian Gray? Is that his name?" asked Lord Henry, walking across the studio towards Basil Hallward.

"Yes, that is his name. I didn't intend to tell it to you."

"But why not?"

"Oh, I can't explain. When I like people immensely, I never tell their names to any one. It is like surrendering a part of them. I have grown to love secrecy. It seems to be the one thing that can make modern life mysterious or marvelous to us. The commonest thing is delightful if one only hides it. When I leave town now I never tell my people where I am going. If I did, I would lose all my pleasure. It is a silly habit, I dare say, but somehow it seems to bring a great deal of romance into one's life. I suppose you think me awfully foolish about it?"

"Not at all," answered Lord Henry, "not at all, my dear Basil. You seem to forget that I am married, and the one charm of marriage is that it makes a life of deception absolutely necessary for both parties. I never know where my wife is, and my wife never knows what I am doing. When we meet—we do meet occasionally, when we dine out together, or go down to the Duke's—we tell each other the most absurd stories with the most serious faces. My wife is very good at it—much better, in fact, than I am. She never gets confused over her dates, and I always do. But when she does find me out, she makes no row at all. I sometimes wish she would; but she merely laughs at me."

"I hate the way you talk about your married life, Harry," said Basil Hallward, strolling towards the door that led into the garden. "I believe that you are really a very good husband, but that you are thoroughly ashamed of your own virtues. You are an extraordinary fellow. You never say a moral thing, and you never do a wrong thing. Your cynicism is simply a pose."

"Being natural is simply a pose, and the most irritating pose I know," cried Lord Henry, laughing; and the two young men went out into the garden together and ensconced themselves on a long bamboo seat that stood in the shade of a tall laurel bush. The sunlight slipped over the polished leaves. In the grass, white daisies were tremulous.

After a pause, Lord Henry pulled out his watch. "I am afraid I must be going, Basil," he murmured, "and before I go, I insist on your answering a question I put to you some time ago."

"What is that?" said the painter, keeping his eyes fixed on the ground.

"You know quite well."

"I do not, Harry."

"Well, I will tell you what it is. I want you to explain to me why you won't exhibit Dorian Gray's picture. I want the real reason."

"I told you the real reason."

"No, you did not. You said it was because there was too much of yourself in it. Now, that is childish."

"Harry," said Basil Hallward, looking him straight in the face, "every portrait that is painted with feeling is a portrait of the artist, not of the sitter. The sitter is merely the accident, the occasion. It is not he who is revealed by the painter; it is rather the painter who, on the coloured canvas, reveals himself. The reason I will not exhibit this picture is that I am afraid that I have shown in it the secret of my own soul."

Lord Henry laughed. "And what is that?" he asked.

"I will tell you," said Hallward; but an expression of perplexity came over his face.

"I am all expectation, Basil," continued his companion, glancing at him.

"Oh, there is really very little to tell, Harry," answered the painter; "and I am afraid you will hardly understand it. Perhaps you will hardly believe it."

Lord Henry smiled, and leaning down, plucked a pink-petalled daisy from the grass and examined it. "I am quite sure I shall understand it," he replied, gazing intently at the little golden, white-feathered disk, "and as for believing things, I can believe anything, provided that it is quite incredible."

The wind shook some blossoms from the trees, and the heavy lilac-blooms, with their clustering stars, moved to and fro in the languid air. A grasshopper began to chirrup by the wall, and like a blue thread a long thin dragon-fly floated past on its brown gauze wings. Lord Henry felt as if he could hear Basil Hallward's heart beating, and wondered what was coming.

"The story is simply this," said the painter after some time. "Two months ago I went to a crush at Lady Brandon's. You know we poor artists have to show ourselves in society from time to time, just to remind the public that we are not savages. With an evening coat and a white tie, as you told me once, anybody, even a stock-broker, can gain a reputation for being civilized. Well, after I had been in the room about ten minutes, talking to huge overdressed dowagers and tedious academicians, I suddenly became conscious that some one was looking at me. I turned half-way round and saw

Dorian Gray for the first time. When our eyes met, I felt that I was growing pale. A curious sensation of terror came over me. I knew that I had come face to face with some one whose mere personality was so fascinating that, if I allowed it to do so, it would absorb my whole nature, my whole soul, my very art itself. I did not want any external influence in my life. You know yourself, Harry, how independent I am by nature. I have always been my own master; had at least always been so, till I met Dorian Gray. Then—but I don't know how to explain it to you. Something seemed to tell me that I was on the verge of a terrible crisis in my life. I had a strange feeling that fate had in store for me exquisite joys and exquisite sorrows. I grew afraid and turned to quit the room. It was not conscience that made me do so: it was a sort of cowardice. I take no credit to myself for trying to escape."

"Conscience and cowardice are really the same things, Basil. Conscience is the trade-name of the firm. That is all."

"I don't believe that, Harry, and I don't believe you do either. However, whatever was my motive—and it may have been pride, for I used to be very proud—I certainly struggled to the door. There, of course, I stumbled against Lady Brandon. 'You are not going to run away so soon, Mr. Hallward?' she screamed out. You know her curiously shrill voice?"

"Yes; she is a peacock in everything but beauty," said Lord Henry, pulling the daisy to bits with his long nervous fingers.

"I could not get rid of her. She brought me up to royalties, and people with stars and garters, and elderly ladies with gigantic tiaras and parrot noses. She spoke of me as her dearest friend. I had only met her once before, but she took it into her head to lionize me. I believe some picture of mine had made a great success at the time, at least had been chattered about in the penny newspapers, which is the nineteenth-century standard of immortality. Suddenly I found myself face to face with the young man whose personality had so strangely stirred me. We were quite close, almost touching. Our eyes met again. It was reckless of me, but I asked Lady Brandon to introduce me to him. Perhaps it was not so reckless, after all. It was simply inevitable. We would have spoken to each other without any introduction. I am sure of that. Dorian told me so afterwards. He, too, felt that we were destined to know each other."

"And how did Lady Brandon describe this wonderful young man?" asked his companion. "I know she goes in for giving a rapid precis of all her guests. I remember her bringing me up to a truculent and red-faced old gentleman covered all over with orders and ribbons, and hissing into my ear, in a tragic whisper which must have been perfectly audible to everybody in the room, the most astounding details. I simply fled. I like to find out people for myself. But Lady Brandon treats her guests exactly as an auctioneer treats his goods. She either explains them entirely away, or tells one everything about them except what one wants to know."

"Poor Lady Brandon! You are hard on her, Harry!" said Hallward listlessly.

"My dear fellow, she tried to found a salon, and only succeeded in opening a restaurant. How could I admire her? But tell me, what did she say about Mr. Dorian Gray?"

"Oh, something like, 'Charming boy—poor dear mother and I absolutely inseparable. Quite forget what he does—afraid he—doesn't do anything—oh, yes, plays the piano—or is it the violin, dear Mr. Gray?' Neither of us could help laughing, and we became friends at once."

"Laughter is not at all a bad beginning for a friendship, and it is far the best ending for one," said the young lord, plucking another daisy.

Hallward shook his head. "You don't understand what friendship is, Harry," he murmured—"or what enmity is, for that matter. You like every one; that is to say, you are indifferent to every one."

"How horribly unjust of you!" cried Lord Henry, tilting his hat back and looking up at the little clouds that, like ravelled skeins of glossy white silk, were drifting across the hollowed turquoise of the summer sky. "Yes; horribly unjust of you. I make a great difference between people. I choose my friends for their good looks, my acquaintances for their good characters, and my enemies for their good intellects. A man cannot be too careful in the choice of his enemies. I have not got one who is a fool. They are all men of some intellectual power, and consequently they all appreciate me. Is that very vain of me? I think it is rather vain."

"I should think it was, Harry. But according to your category I must be merely an acquaintance."

"My dear old Basil, you are much more than an acquaintance."

"And much less than a friend. A sort of brother, I suppose?"

"Oh, brothers! I don't care for brothers. My elder brother won't die, and my younger brothers seem never to do anything else."

"Harry!" exclaimed Hallward, frowning.

"My dear fellow, I am not quite serious. But I can't help detesting my relations. I suppose it comes from the fact that none of us can stand other people having the same faults as ourselves. I quite sympathize with the rage of the English democracy against what they call the vices of the upper orders. The masses feel that drunkenness, stupidity, and immorality should be their own special property, and that if any one of us makes an ass of himself, he is poaching on their preserves. When poor Southwark got into the divorce court, their indignation was quite magnificent. And yet I don't suppose that ten per cent of the proletariat live correctly."

"I don't agree with a single word that you have said, and, what is more, Harry, I feel sure you don't either."

Lord Henry stroked his pointed brown beard and tapped the toe of his patent-leather boot with a tasselled ebony cane. "How English you are Basil! That is the second time you have made that observation. If one puts forward an idea to a true Englishman—always a rash thing to do—he never dreams of considering whether the idea is right or wrong. The only thing he considers of any importance is whether one believes it oneself. Now, the value of an idea has nothing whatsoever to do with the sincerity of the man who expresses it. Indeed, the probabilities are that the more insincere the man is, the more purely intellectual will the idea be, as in that case it will not be coloured by either his wants, his desires, or his prejudices.

However, I don't propose to discuss politics, sociology, or metaphysics with you. I like persons better than principles, and I like persons with no principles better than anything else in the world. Tell me more about Mr. Dorian Gray. How often do you see him?"

"Every day. I couldn't be happy if I didn't see him every day. He is absolutely necessary to me."

"How extraordinary! I thought you would never care for anything but your art."

"He is all my art to me now," said the painter gravely. "I sometimes think, Harry, that there are only two eras of any importance in the world's history. The first is the appearance of a new medium for art, and the second is the appearance of a new personality for art also. What the invention of oil-painting was to the Venetians, the face of Antinous was to late Greek sculpture, and the face of Dorian Gray will some day be to me. It is not merely that I paint from him, draw from him, sketch from him. Of course, I have done all that. But he is much more to me than a model or a sitter. I won't tell you that I am dissatisfied with what I have done of him, or that his beauty is such that art cannot express it. There is nothing that art cannot express, and I know that the work I have done, since I met Dorian Gray, is good work, is the best work of my life. But in some curious way—I wonder will you understand me? —his personality has suggested to me an entirely new manner in art, an entirely new mode of style. I see things differently, I think of them differently. I can now recreate life in a way that was hidden from me before. 'A dream of form in days of thought'—who is it who says that? I forget; but it is what Dorian Gray has been to me. The merely visible presence of this lad—for he seems to me little more than a lad, though he is really over twenty—his merely visible presence—ah! I wonder can you realize all that that means? Unconsciously he defines for me the lines of a fresh school, a school that is to have in it all the passion of the romantic spirit, all the perfection of the spirit that is Greek. The harmony of soul and body—how much that is! We in our madness have separated the two, and have invented a realism that is vulgar, an ideality that is void. Harry! if you only knew what Dorian Gray is to me! You remember that landscape of mine, for which Agnew offered me such a huge price but which I would not part with? It is one of the best things I have ever done. And why is it so? Because, while I was painting it, Dorian Gray sat beside me. Some subtle influence passed from him to me, and for the first time in my life I saw in the plain woodland the wonder I had always looked for and always missed."

"Basil, this is extraordinary! I must see Dorian Gray."

Hallward got up from the seat and walked up and down the garden. After some time he came back. "Harry," he said, "Dorian Gray is to me simply a motive in art. You might see nothing in him. I see everything in him. He is never more present in my work than when no image of him is there. He is a suggestion, as I have said, of a new manner. I find him in the curves of certain lines, in the loveliness and subtleties of certain colours. That is all."

"Then why won't you exhibit his portrait?" asked Lord Henry.

"Because, without intending it, I have put into it some expression of all this curious artistic idolatry, of which, of course, I have never cared to speak to him. He knows nothing about it. He shall never know anything about it. But the world might guess it, and I will not bare my soul to their shallow prying eyes. My heart shall never be put under their microscope. There is too much of myself in the thing, Harry—too much of myself!"

"Poets are not so scrupulous as you are. They know how useful passion is for publication. Nowadays a broken heart will run to many editions."

"I hate them for it," cried Hallward. "An artist should create beautiful things, but should put nothing of his own life into them. We live in an age when men treat art as if it were meant to be a form of autobiography. We have lost the abstract sense of beauty. Some day I will show the world what it is; and for that reason the world shall never see my portrait of Dorian Gray."

"I think you are wrong, Basil, but I won't argue with you. It is only the intellectually lost who ever argue. Tell me, is Dorian Gray very fond of you?"

The painter considered for a few moments. "He likes me," he answered after a pause; "I know he likes me. Of course I flatter him dreadfully. I find a strange pleasure in saying things to him that I know I shall be sorry for having said. As a rule, he is charming to me, and we sit in the studio and talk of a thousand things. Now and then, however, he is horribly thoughtless, and seems to take a real delight in giving me pain. Then I feel, Harry, that I have given away my whole soul to some one who treats it as if it were a flower to put in his coat, a bit of decoration to charm his vanity, an ornament for a summer's day."

"Days in summer, Basil, are apt to linger," murmured Lord

Henry. "Perhaps you will tire sooner than he will. It is a sad thing to think of, but there is no doubt that genius lasts longer than beauty. That accounts for the fact that we all take such pains to over-edu cate ourselves. In the wild struggle for existence, we want to have something that endures, and so we fill our minds with rubbish and facts, in the silly hope of keeping our place. The thoroughly well-informed man—that is the modern ideal. And the mind of the thoroughly well-informed man is a dreadful thing. It is like a bric-a-brac shop, all monsters and dust, with everything priced above its proper value. I think you will tire first, all the same. Some day you will look at your friend, and he will seem to you to be a little out of drawing, or you won't like his tone of colour, or something. You will bitterly reproach him in your own heart, and seriously think that he has behaved very badly to you. The next time he calls, you will be perfectly cold and indifferent. It will be a great pity, for it will alter you. What you have told me is quite a romance, a romance of art one might call it, and the worst of having a romance of any kind is that it leaves one so unromantic."

"Harry, don't talk like that. As long as I live, the personality of Dorian Gray will dominate me. You can't feel what I feel. You change too often."

"Ah, my dear Basil, that is exactly why I can feel it. Those who are faithful know only the trivial side of love: it is the faithless who know love's tragedies." And Lord Henry struck a light on a dainty silver case and began to smoke a cigarette with a self-conscious and satisfied air, as if he had summed up the world in a phrase. There was a rustle of chirruping sparrows in the green lacquer leaves of the ivy, and the blue cloud-shadows chased themselves across the grass like swallows. How pleasant it was in the garden! And how delightful other people's emotions were! —much more delightful than their ideas, it seemed to him. One's own soul, and the passions of one's friends—those were the fascinating things in life. He pictured to himself with silent amusement the tedious luncheon that he had missed by staying so long with Basil Hallward. Had he gone to his aunt's, he would have been sure to have met Lord Goodbody there, and the whole conversation would have been about the feeding of the poor and the necessity for model lodging-houses. Each class would have preached the importance of those virtues, for whose exercise there was no necessity in their own lives. The rich would have spoken on the value of thrift, and the idle grown eloquent over the dignity of labour. It was charming to have escaped all that! As he thought of his aunt, an idea seemed to strike him. He turned to Hallward and said, "My dear fellow, I have just remembered."

"Remembered what, Harry?"

"Where I heard the name of Dorian Gray."

"Where was it?" asked Hallward, with a slight frown.

"Don't look so angry, Basil. It was at my aunt, Lady Agatha's. She told me she had discovered a wonderful young man who was going to help her in the East End, and that his name was Dorian Gray. I am bound to state that she never told me he was good-looking. Women have no appreciation of good looks; at least, good women have not. She said that he was very earnest and had a beautiful nature. I at once pictured to myself a creature with spectacles and lank hair, horribly freckled, and tramping about on huge feet. I wish I had known it was your friend."

"I am very glad you didn't, Harry."

"Why?"

"I don't want you to meet him."

"You don't want me to meet him?"

"No."

"Mr. Dorian Gray is in the studio, sir," said the butler, coming into the garden.

"You must introduce me now," cried Lord Henry, laughing.

The painter turned to his servant, who stood blinking in the sunlight. "Ask Mr. Gray to wait, Parker: I shall be in in a few moments." The man bowed and went up the walk.

Then he looked at Lord Henry. "Dorian Gray is my dearest friend," he said. "He has a simple and a beautiful nature. Your aunt was quite right in what she said of him. Don't spoil him. Don't try to influence him. Your influence would be bad. The world is wide, and has many marvelous people in it. Don't take away from me the one person who gives to my art whatever charm it possesses: my life as an artist depends on him. Mind, Harry, I trust you." He spoke very slowly, and the words seemed wrung out of him almost against his will.

"What nonsense you talk!" said Lord Henry, smiling, and taking Hallward by the arm, he almost led him into the house.